Pilot of Varying Lights: Early Stories

By the author of
FANTASTIC TRAVELOGUE

Pilot of Varying Lights:
Early Stories
S. Dorman

"The Space Shuttle Discovery and its seven-member STS-120 crew head toward Earth-orbit and a scheduled link-up with the International Space Station. Liftoff from Kennedy Space Center's launch pad 39A occurred at 11:38:19 a.m. (EDT). Onboard are astronauts Pam Melroy, commander; George Zamka, pilot; Scott Parazynski, Stephanie Wilson, Doug Wheelock, European Space Agency's (ESA) Paolo Nespoli and Daniel Tani, all mission specialists. [Image} NASA; edited by jjron (tilt corrected) - http://spaceflight.nasa.gov/gallery/images/shuttle/sts-120/html/sts120-s-028.html. Public Domain."

There is no water in oxygen, no water in hydrogen: it comes bubbling fresh from the imagination of the living God, rushing from under the great white throne of the glacier. The very thought of it makes one gasp with an elemental joy no metaphysician can analyze. [T]his live thing which, if I might, I would have running through my room, yea, babbling along my table—this water is ... its own truth, and is therein the truth of God.
— *George MacDonald*

Table of Contents

Magma's Net

When the planets first accreted and spun into orbit, Plasma helped create a space-sea of electrified particles for them to float on. She did this by spending much of her time shooting about through the twisting halls of the Sun, her radiant train of electrons and ions following. After a trip of twenty thousand years (give or take a few thousand), these radiant particles of her train would reach the cooler sun-surface. Then they would slip minutely through Photos' fences to enter the great space-sea. It would take only minutes for these rays to reach nearby planets.

For long Plasma was content to rush up and down the fiery winding hallways, making sure her particles got to the fences. But, later, when every turning became too familiar and the way to the fences got old, Plasma became discontented. Then the creativity went out of her work. Finally, Plasma was bored with the Sun.

I need a new situation. Something artistic and exciting, to match my zingy arresting temperament.

So she gathered up her dazzling train and shot up through hot gases to the light-fence. Having heard rumors of Plasma's dissatisfaction, bright Photos and beautiful Chromos came out to meet her.

"Photos, Chromos ... you're just in time to bid me goodbye."

"Plasma, no!" Chromos, keeper of the color fence, softly exclaimed. Her flame-shaped gradating colors intensified with distress. And Photos urged, "Let us talk it over," wondering where in the *Cosmos* Plasma wanted to go.

"Talk schmalk. It's my life, you know." In her set face ran the buzzing shooting pulse of her nature.

Chromos' glowing colors darkened slightly in perplexity. "But why, Plasma, dear?" she asked. "The Sun is source for all physical life in the solar system. We are so fortunate to share in his vast work." Even Photos dimmed a touch and he stood in thought, wondering how to dissuade her.

But Plasma was impatient with them. "Photos, charge Umbra to open the gates. I want through your light-fence—now!"

But the man of light admonished her. "Electric one, we all have minds of our own, yet we are limited by the laws of the Cosmos. Remember this as you go."

A bored expression in her eyes, Plasma looked up at the soaring brilliant light-fence. "Sermons, my friends, all sermons."

So, failing to convince her, Photos went up through the fence in a tremendous cloud of calcium vapor. A moment later, black Umbra began opening the dark gates in the light-fence. So powerful was Plasma's rapid exit that a violent storm soared upwards, sending her out on a radiant blast into the sun-system.

How mighty was Plasma! Her fast-moving electrons and slower ions came on behind, a vast cloud of poisonous gas.

Grieving Chromos sent her maidens, the Sun Prominences, flying like scarlet streamers, after Plasma. She hoped they might persuade her to come back. But Plasma was swift. The Prominences could not catch her, and so fell quickly back to the Sun.

Then, rushing through the sun-system, Plasma suddenly saw that she had no plan beyond escape. Looking this way and that, she sought a destination. Perhaps one of those young orbs—as she called the planets— perhaps one might accommodate her. She spied blue earth floating dead ahead in the black space-sea. Smiling she surged forward, drawing a deadly radiant train of electrons and ions behind her. She did not think of the damage that would be done by such an onslaught of her deadly radiation. Maybe she simply forgot about the delicate atmospheric fences surrounding earth.

Fortunately Magma, the keeper of earth's inner, molten iron-oxide fence, had been on watch when dark spots appeared as Umbra opened the sun-gates. Magma saw Plasma shoot from the Sun. Thus he was ready when she came rushing toward earth. He spun out an invisible net, far larger than earth and specially magnetized. Unraveling from earth's geomagnetic poles, it tumbled around and through atmospheric fences, surrounding the blue orb.

And, though strong, intelligent and creative. Plasma could not see what was invisible to her. She passed into his magnetic net along with all her electrons and ions. How she struggled and kicked, and pulled on Magma's net! Fiercely she glowed—green, yellow, lavender, red. Plasma thrashed and thrashed in the buzzing net. Her glowing rays moving and changing shape.

Magma looked up at her display, delighted, and laughed. "Holy Cosmos! child, but you can dance!"

Wood Mother

It is night in the woods and the air is still and cold. The moon is away. Comes a sound of scampering, then silence. Nothing moves for some moments.

From a hole in a log buried under a pile of sodden leaves, a pale snout emerges. Its whiskers tremble and go still. After a pause the long head of a opossum follows. Her convex black eyes peer through the tangle. Nothing threatening out here. Opossum climbs out of the day's lodgings and ambles into the woods.

Head down, flat footed, a-foraging she goes. Her coat is pale gray but her tail is pink and scaly, rat-like. Opossum is now on her way to the spring for water, however, a few investigative side trips are always in order. The little marsupial shambles from a thicket, her bat-like naked ears pricked for every sound. At the base of an old pumpkin pine she nuzzles into a broken knot to grub out some dormant ants. Frozen wood-ants taste and crunch like frozen cranberries.

Backing away, jaws still crunching the last mouthful, she gets scent and hears a clicking sound. Opossum has never heard this noise before but it rouses something in her. She turns. A male opossum is there. Again he addresses her with a series of clicks. Now, standing, they joined in brief coupling, then go their separate ways.

The female opossum finds the spring and drinks thirstly. The rest of the night is spent meandering along, nosing for edibles in the crannies of the forest.

On the twelfth day following her encounter with a male, the previously mild winter stirs up a howling storm. It blows the rest of the day and into the night.

Opossum holes up in a dilapidated shack that quakes with every surge of the wind. The blast goes on and on and she becomes restless. Her uterus contracts painfully as she circles inside the shack, sometimes stopping to stand on her hind feet before dropping to all fours again.

Outside, the banging of a loose board persists. Snow blows in through chinks in the slats.

Now she stands in the corner bent forward, toiling. A tiny embryonic animal appears at her vaginal opening and Opossum licks it free of its wet covering. Tinier than a honeybee, the faltering slick little creature begins pulling itself up along a pathway licked flat on the fur of its mother. There is no other assistance for the newborn that claws upward on strong forelegs toward the pouch upon Opossum's middle. Its hind legs are so under-developed that they are useless. When safely inside, it gropes for a nipple and latches on.

Now Opossum licks free another one, and it starts on the same perilous journey. There comes a cracking noise and the young mother is knocked over by a falling plank. When she regains her birth giving posture, the second little opossum is gone, shortly to perish in the rubble on the floor.

In quick succession seven others are born. Afterwards Opossum's pouch is full of her snuggling sucklings. Exhausted, bedraggled, she curls up under a fallen board and drops off to sleep. But outside the storm still beats on the listing shack.

In the night following the storm, Opossum continues her roving habits but now she is not alone.

Spring comes slowly at first. Pickings for Opossum are lean. So she eats what is most plentiful—carrion.

Recalling the previous night's dinner, one wide awake April evening, she travels down toward a pond. Opossum's slightly bulging pouch will protect her babies from drowning while she wades.

The babies are 36 days old and have had use of their hind of legs for two weeks. She can feel them nudging her belly as they nurse.

Weaving through the long sedge on the bank of the pond she hears the whooshing of wings overhead, recognizing danger. Her little heart ticking, she plunges into the water, narrowly escaping the spring-trap claws of a great horned owl. Opossum swims silently underwater for some moments. When she surfaces the owl is gone. Head out of the water, front and rear feet moving in unison, she makes her way back across the pond. Now in the shallows, and stirring clouds of silt in the dark water, she rummages out her crayfish from under a rock shelf. Then she climbs heavily out of the water.

May arrives sweetly and Opossum is able to add more plant life to her diet. Her furry babies are now so big that they lounge outside her pouch on warm days while she sleeps. Lazily, they continue to suckle.

Rambling in the open one night she discovers a patch of early black raspberries and stops to rifle through them. Now she smells danger, a bobcat, and scurries into the bushes.

The stubble-tailed cat pounces late but manages to grab her hindquarters. Its fierce claws rake deep down her rump. Opossum yields to a death feint, falling curled on her side. Her babies remain hidden beneath in her pouch.

Puzzled by the stiffness of its prey, the bobcat releases its hold. This opossum shows only the signs of death. Its breath has stopped. Its mouth open, its tongue hangs out. The bobcat sniffs at it, paws it once or twice then turns away in search of live prey.

It is some minutes before the marsupial regains consciousness. She stirs sluggishly coming out of the feint. Struggling to stand, Opossum feels searing pain. She looks about dazedly as inside her pouch the baby's squirm and kick. Now they tumble out. All but one have managed to keep hold on the long nipples. From the ground this lost little opossum makes sneezing sounds, fumbling for its mother. It catches hold of her rear leg and mounts over her sticky wounds to reach its brothers and sisters. Swift pain pierces through Opossum.

Her babies bumping on the ground, trembling, she drags herself into a thicket where she collapses. This cover will help protect her babies. Now she bides the night and part of the next day, thirsting.

Babies suckle, lounging in shadows outside her pouch, as Opossum falls into a strange state. Waves of heat and whirring sensations, probe her little body. Shards of nightmare pierce her. Someone is lifting her, babies clinging. A face like that of an owl looms large above her, voicing noises. Bitter water is trickling on her tongue. She has become a baby opossum: blindly, wetly climbing out of a fever on strong fore claws, dragging her useless hind legs. She routs for the place of keeping and the nipple of nurture. Opossum sleeps. When she wakes, the day is too bright. She is weak, worn, resting. That too-flat face of the owl peers at her, grinning. He makes owl sounds.

"Little good mother wakes." The native Delaware Indian says this, nodding.

He gives Opossum her water in a clay bowl. Opossum stands to drink, her babies twisting, clutching with hind feet and rat-like tails.

It is night. Opossum stirs in the refreshing darkness. Her senses are alert. Her whiskers quiver. She stands, shaking herself shaking off. Now sitting back on her haunches to scratch an annoying tick, she discovers an uncomfortable stiffness.

But suddenly she is very hungry and realizes that the woods are full of food. Off she ambles, babies upon her back. Moldering old logs harbor lots of insects. And there might be a wild cherry tree or two for the climbing.

The Hewer

Ave Slaughter was in the woods with his orphaned nephew Jedidiah. They had come up the Chippewa from Eau Clair in search of white pine. On their backs were enough supplies and equipment for a month's surveying, and in Slaughter's calloused palm lay a compass attached to a gold-filled chain. He got a fix that agreed with his sun reading and slid the instrument back into the pocket of his canvas pants. Southeast was the river—all the transportation he needed to get his logs to the mill a hundred miles down stream on the Mississippi. West and north were the pines. Where they stood now was as good a place as any to make camp. Slaughter told his mind to Jedidiah, and the grateful youth let his pack and pole-ax drop to the ground. But his work was beginning.

"Fall four saplings and lash'em for the wigwam," said Slaughter. "Then start on camp. I'm going for hemlock bark." By evening they had a hemlock wigwam, beans and saltpork simmering in the iron fry pan over a bed of hot coals, and coffee in the pot sitting off to one side, boiling away.

"Tomorrow we'll check the snares, Jed. Get some fresh rabbit or squirrel to go with the beans."

The youth spooned pork and beans onto the graniteware and handed it to Ave. He spooned a plateful for himself then poured out coffee for them both. Together they sat back and supped. Presently, coffee in him and the work of the day done, Jed was buoyant.

He fed the fire, a bit then sat down and began picking his teeth with a splinter. "Tell me a tale, Big Ave."

Slaughter grunted, swished the grounds around in the bottom of his cup and tossed them out. He looked up at the campfire's jumping lights and shadows cast high in the silent trees. Then he cleared his throat and began.

"It was '30 or '31, in the winter on the Menominee River. A fur trader named Farnsworth built a sawmill there." He stopped and chuckled, remembering the times he'd used dynamite to move men.

"The Menominee didn't want no sawmill planted in the woods, having no use like we do for lumbering. A delegation of fifteen or so came—very polite—and told him to leave or be killed. Well, he rolled out a keg of powder, opened it and stuck the butt end of a lighted candle smack into it. The Indians shifted a bit where they sat.

" 'You are braves of Menominee; I am a brave. We'll sit here and dare death together.' Then Farnsworth straddled the keg, and they all watched the candle shrink, the flame inching toward powder.

"An Indian stood and, stooping, went out the door. Soon another followed, and another. Finally there was but one Menominee and Farnsworth, setting there to meet death. Then the remaining brave rose with dignity. Out he walked. Farnsworth wet his thumb and finger and pressed out the flame.

"Gained him a reputation." Slaughter winked. "Of course it was himself told the story."

The campfire sent waves of amber light across Jed's awed features. "Tell me another!"

The middle-aged man filled up the evening with stories. He told of the Aroostook War in 1838 and '39 when Maine toted brass cannons into the hills; when the mighty white pines of the northeast were in dispute, before Canada and Maine knew their borders.

"All that for a tree?"

"Not just a tree, boy. White pine. He soars head and shoulders above the others—his base sometimes six, eight feet through. Sit under one—you'll hear him sing like a choir."

He stood, stretching and yawning. "You'll see what I mean tomorrow. Get to bed. You got to keep wholesome."

Jed gave his uncle's back a puzzled look. Then he shrugged. He stood and brushed off his new canvas pants, bought for him in Eau Claire for his new job with Uncle Ave—now his only kin.

Morning was dim in the woods when they woke. Breakfast was the same as the previous night's meal, quickly consumed. Ave was in a hurry to locate the trees. They headed north, climbing a long steady grade above camp.

When they reached the crest the man gave Jed a boost up a shellbark hickory.

Slaughter yelled. "What do you see?!"

The voice drifted down. "Trees...."

Patience intact, Ave hollered, "Do you see the white pine?"

Silence.

Then, "I see'em, I see'em! Head and shoulders above the others, like you said!"

Later, through the trees, Slaughter got a glimpse of the broad trunks. He heard wind walking in their numberless branches. Approaching, he swallowed hard and reached absently into his pocket for the remainder of a plug of Climax. Slaughter walked the deep needled duff among the trunks, his mind rapidly calculating. Almost a stand in size, it was the largest grove he had ever seen.

"Jedidiah!" he called. "Were those other clumps as big as this?... His gaze searched uneasily through the gloom. "Jedidiah!"

"I'm here, Big Ave," came the small voice.

The man turned. Jed, considerably dwarfed, sat beneath one lofty white pine. His boyish head lolled against the hoary old bole. High above, the moving boughs intoned.

"You're right, Big Ave. He does sing."

At a boarding house on Lumber St. in Eau Clair a sign neatly read: *Rooms for Gentlemen.*

As they approached the supper table Slaughter warned Jed, "I'll be going out tonight. You'll be safe in bed—getting your spelling and numbers." He recruited two choppers right at the boarding house table, then the camp boss went to the saloons.

With a few friendly words, some loud guffaws, and a hand to his drawstring pouch, he entered Grand's. He fingered the wad his bosses at Winona had backed him with and announced drinks for every logger in the place, then he set up office at the oaken bar. Ave Slaughter was hiring for Pulp and Paper.

Toward morning, in a corner of some saloon, he came upon black-bearded "Ten-foot" Matisse. The son of a Frenchman, the teamster was named for his ability to toss logs, boulders, even his own horse such distances. He was rotund, unmovable. His arms were like oak limbs, his thighs like tamarack stumps. He sat at the table quietly drinking.

"Matisse," signaled Ave. "Mind if I pull up a chair?"

The big man assented with a move of his stout hand. "What're you drinking?"

But Slaughter said, "I'm buying tonight—or rather Pulp and Paper of Beef Slough is buying."

Ten-foot relinquished a thick chuckle. "Nothing like a lumber baron to get a town off the skids in the fall."

Slaughter agreed sociably. "How come you're still in the dough?"

Matisse ignored the question. "What's the main chance this year?"

Slaughter told him about his find north of Eau Clair, west of the Chippewa. Solemnity lit Ten-foot's eyes. "I wondered when they'd get around to it. "I've seen those trees."

Both men sat like statues, wondering. Had they seen the living ancestry of white pine? Maybe every such pine had hailed from there.

Slaughter broke the spell with a sigh. "We'll fall 'em all." He was remembering the decimation of the white pine northern forests in Maine after the hewer came through ... the stumps stretching to the desolate horizon...."

"Yeah, but think of the fight they'll give the hewers and cant-dogs. Those poor boogers'll have the devil getting the old kings on those two-sleds."

They talked on, Slaughter never quite asking Matisse to join up. At last he pushed his glass away and stood. "Good seeing you, Ten-foot." He nodded and turned away.

"Slaughter," said Matisse, as the boss was about to pass through the door. "I'll be there when you pull out. Me and the team."

"Right," the other replied.

Daybreak was stirring the breezes when Slaughter entered the boarding house.

It was noon through chinks in the blind, and there was a soft rapping at the bedroom door.

"Jedidiah, answer the door," muttered Ave Slaughter from bed. But the rapping continued.

Tap tap tap.

Ave flung out an arm, groping for his trousers.

Tap tap tap.

"Aw right!" he croaked, dragging his pants up. He crossed the room, noting Jedidiah's absence and the smell of slops from the corner bucket. He flung open the door.

A puckered little old woman stood there, wrapped in a shawl, leaning on a cane. Ave stared down on her.

"I've come for the boy," she said. Her voice quavered slightly.

He gave her a puzzled frown.

"You know," she prompted. It was softly spoken.

A flush of dread roared through him. He stammered. "But you don't look—I don't know what—what you mean." His mind cast wildly about for some stall. *This can't be her.*

"You shouldn't lie, man."

"Don't—don't take him just yet—I'm sure something more needs done before—that."

There was a pause. The old woman stood very still, leaning on that cane. Then she said, "Yes, that's true. Something more could be done, so you'll have your time. Just remember, Jedidiah is mine."

Trembling slightly, Ave closed the door. He went and sat on the bed, looking down at his work-hardened fingers, remembering the barren hospital room and someone beloved lying in the iron bedstead.

When he got back to the woods, Jedidiah looked up the beaver colony he'd discovered during the survey. His uncle was pre-occupied with setting up camp for a hundred men—and with some private worry or so it seemed—so when his chores were done, Jed spent hours in an old maple reading the primer and watching the beavers prepare for winter. The air was cool and full of the smell of leaf mold.

The older beavers had dug a trench three rods into the woods in order to reach the smaller hardwoods they used in dam building. From his perch Jed watched them fall and limb cottonwood, birch and maple, floating them down to the creek where other beavers waited to steer the trunks toward a dam. The younger beavers gathered food, submerging tender stems beneath the surface of the pond not far from the lodge. From time to time Jed chuckled softly at the comic maneuvers of certain beavers. He was getting to know them one by one.

Whenever a tree fell he noticed that the beavers would waddle to the pond and dive in. Why did all the beavers hide when one tree fell?

In time he found out. A tree fell and the beavers dove for cover. Then a slinky red weasel came picking its way through the undergrowth. A smallish critter, but Jed realized it was a danger to the kits. The weasel nosed around the pond then wandered away. Before long Jed spied sets of nostrils and buck teeth breaking the surface of the water.

The chopping crews were out falling white pine by the score.

Thoughts of the woman—and Jed—bothered Slaughter as he walked under the tall trees to watch the crews' progress. He would try his pole-ax a time or two, to rid himself of trouble.

He came upon the first crew: the hewer or head chopper, second chopper, and swamper. They looked like toy loggers in the light-speckled shadows beneath towering pines. The hewer "heyed" the boss and kept on working, his strokes echoing in the woods.

"See that, boss?" The swamper indicated a heavy crooked branch lying not far from the hewer.

"Widow-maker," grunted Ave.

"Spiteful, this one is," said the swamper. "Threw it down with no warning, no sound."

"Yeah, she won't give up—if that's being spiteful." The hewer spared these words as a volley of sweat flew off his back while his bit sank deep into the cut.

Slaughter gazed up the straight firm trunk in admiration. The hewer and second chopper were almost half-way through on either side, but the great pine was unmoving, powerfully scenting the woods with pine resin.

"Get the killig pole," Slaughter said to the swamper without glancing away.

The chopping was nearly finished. Slaughter angled the pole into the undercut and began shoving with all his muscle. Axe strokes still flying, the tree began to stir. Groaning. Like a mountain, it turned slowly.

"Damnation!" yelled the hewer. "She's gone wrong!"

For an instant they stared dumbly as the mighty white, still standing, shifted down off its pinnacle. The loggers threw down their axes and ran.

Whooshing and cracking it fell. But silence came too soon.

Looking back through the dim forest, they saw the ground empty below. In the green light just opened, pine needles sifted down. They hurried back to it, gazing upwards, and saw the tree cradled in the crossed trunks of two other white pines.

"She's laughing, I'll swear," said the hewer and let fly a string of tobacco juice.

In the evening, Ave stood nigh the woods not far from the shanty he shared with his nephew. Jed was long asleep. In the bigger bunk shanty next door, rowdy thumps, yells, and singing accompanied the vigorous outpouring of an old squeeze box.

Yet Ave could still sense the forest quiet. Crickets, not yet done in by frost, trilled away in the underwood. He sighed deeply, looking around, and presently took a swig of something from his old tin cup.

A pale form was suddenly visible in the distance among the trees. Walking down the path, he recognized the wizened woman who'd stood outside his door at the boarding house in Eau Clair.

Fear leaped up broad in him.

"Mr. Slaughter, I've come for Jedidiah."

That frail croaking voice.

His glance was evasive. "Talk a minute?" She consented and they turned deeper into the woods. He emptied his cup on the ground as they walked. She leaned heavily on her cane.

A stifled cry tore up from his gut. "I need more time—like we agreed. Everything's got to be right before you take him. Then it'll be fittin'. —Won't it?" He grimaced.

The old woman made a sound like a vague breeze sighing through a pinetop. She murmured. "One day they'll stop all this worry."

"...You'll have your time."

He left her there and, relieved, walked back toward camp, fearing to glance back. But passing a tree, he heard a hiss.

"Dynamite-head," said a mocking voice.

Ave turned and shied from the sight.

A decaying corpse sat crosslegged in moon-shadows. Teeming with maggots, its dark rotten flesh scarcely covered its startling white bones.

"I've come for Jedidiah," it mimicked.

White anger surged through the logger. He lifted his leg and emitting a terrible scream rammed his heavy spiked boot into its putrid face. It collapsed and vanished. But the stench lingered.

Ave stomped blindly into camp.

Ten-foot Matisse stood outside the bunk shanty on his way to the barn for a visit with his horses before turning in at the teamsters' camp. He saw the boss returning and hailed him.

"Been fightin'?"

Fresh heat poured through Slaughter. He bowed his head and strode past, muttering, "Just phantoms, is all.

When the chopping crews settled in for the evening beside the hot box stove with a deck of cards at hand, the night sprinklers got into their mackinaws and boots to go out on the coldest job. Jedidiah, watching, decided to go too. He wanted to see what they were up to in the deep-hold of the winter night. The men were leaving: there was no time to get Uncle Ave's permission.

Out through fallen snow they crunched, leaving camp behind. It was good seeing weather, crusty and very cold. After a quarter mile they came out of the woods. The river valley below was a frosty bowl of tree-covered hills curving away southeastward. Down tramped the dark shapes of the three night sprinklers, pickaxes on their broad shoulders, passing the jug back and forth between them. Jed followed a dozen paces behind, the cold north witch biting his cheeks and nose. They passed once more through a tier of woods, ambling downwards. Coming to the clearing, Jed was glad to see immense Matisse waiting with his great four-horse team of Belgian blacks. The breath of their nostrils spurted into the subarctic air and they stood restive.

"Hoo, Ten-foot," hailed Scroggs, handing him the jug.

Jed grinned up at the big man. Matisse reached out a great hand and tussled the boy's hair with his long stout fingers.

"Glad you're along, boy. Keep an eye on Scroggs and let me know if he mistreats my hosses." He sent a meaningful glance at Scroggs.

Then he took a deep thirsty swallow, handed the jug back, and headed through the woods toward the teamster's camp.

Leading these great horses, the night sprinklers walked down a long snow-covered road to the frozen stream below. Jed pulled his stocking cap down snugly and watched as two of the men raised their picks and began chopping through the thick Wisconsin ice. Scroggs hitched three of Matisse's blacks to the huge wooden reservoir ponderously perched on a set of two-sleds, then hooked the pulley rope to the harness of the fourth. As Jed looked on, the man backed the black, lowering the barrel. Gulping, it sank to the bottom. The black pulled, hauling the barrel from the water, bumping up the side of the sprinkler. The man climbed topside and upended the barrel into the reservoir, sloshing its cold water everywhere. Ten hauls and the sprinkler was full.

The men, and the by-now shivering boy, climbed onto the ice-encrusted sprinkler and rode slowly up the hill. One of the men swung his pick-ax down, knocking loose the pegs above each runner. Jed looked down at the water gushing out in twin sprays, washing down the snowy tracks of the two-sled, freezing behind them as they went. Approaching the hilltop he saw a trail of star-lit silver curving down to the stream a half mile below. He began to long for fire and bunk. At the top of the hill he leaped off the sprinkler and headed into the bordering woods.

As he came out on the further side, he scanned the star-glimmering sky. Suddenly a great shadow rose up, starting his heart, blotting out the stars. The ground shook. Jed flung himself down. When he looked up he saw a tremendous axe-man playing with his tool. Hefting a tree in one colossal arm, the giant reached and tossed it among the planets. Down past Jed's head roared a wall of hone steel. It flashed upwards to cleave the far-flung spruce in two. For long moments the giant dallied, demonstrating all the logger's skill with the broad-axe. Then he passed northwards with his great ox, over the foaming, quaking hills.

When he was gone Jed sat up. He scrambled to his feet and ran off among the trees to camp.

Home from a futile search for his nephew, Ave lay staring at the flickering firelight through the grating on the stove. His stomach churned heedlessly. He felt shooting pain in his back. His thoughts jumped from Julia's deathbed to Jed and back again.

Has the old lady come?

The door crashed open. Jed gasped, tumbling breathless into the shanty. "Big Ave! Who walks taller'n white pine?!"

Ave leaned forward on his elbow trying to grasp his nephew's words. Relief overcame him: He fell back, closed his eyes and said, "I give up, who."

They spent the next morning together. Jed took him to see the beaver lodge. Visible only as vague mounds, the once thriving workshop community seemed to sleep under the snow.

"You sure like those deuced beavers," remarked the man as they stood by the pond.

"They're like little loggers only they don't cuss."

Ave laughed.

"Big Ave? ...I'm glad you brought me to the woods with you."

"So'm I Jed."

The two were silent. A branch creaked somewhere high in the trees. The sound was muffled by the snow layer.

"It doesn't bother me as much ... that Mother's gone."

Ave's retort was guarded, shy. "No?"

"Yeah. I know I'm gonna see her again." He smiled some.

Ave swallowed. "That's good." The words sounded silly and numb in his own ears. But Jed did not notice. He smiled again.

In spring the riverhogs came up from the saloons and brothels of Eau Clair and Chippewa Falls. Out on the river they worked in red shirts and kersey trousers, with pike poles and peavys, breaking out the rollways. Up and down the stream men were tending logs away from gravel bars and tangles bordering the river. The stream was thick with tree trunks, and the men loosed more from the banks and roll ways each moment.

Jed was among them on his first walk. Slaughter stood on the bank with Matisse, watching.

Suddenly he started and glanced back across the river. On the opposite bank stood the little woman he felt he could hold off no longer. She looked not a Slaughter but at Jedidiah on the river.

Slaughter's ulcer fired. He leaped onto the logs, bobbing, weaving his way across the moving lumber. But the woman had disappeared. He scoured the banks but found no trace of her. Dismayed, he turned back.

"Phantoms again?" Matisse watched Slaughter's eyes as he hove ashore.

Ave darted him a look. *Could this man believe?* Frowning he turned and watched Jed.

"My sister Julia died in a Chicago hospital last spring... the sugar disease. I was told Jedidiah might develop the symptoms—thirst, lost weight, too many trips to the privy. The doctor said he might even pass out and die—if he's got it."

Slaughter glanced back at Ten-foot then averted his gaze. He reached automatically for a chew, grabbing three fingers' full, pressing it between his gum and cheek. Matisse watched the man's jaw rotate. He shifted his prodigious weight, stroked his curly beard and said nothing.

"Oh hell," barked Slaughter. "A bright, young—ageless—somebody stood by Julia's bed. She gave me the feeling of being straight and firm as a tree." His voice thickened. "She said to me, 'I'll send for her son within the year.' Then she disappeared. And Julia was dead."

Matisse grunted, still stroking his great black beard. "You've seen her again, I suppose?"

"Last summer—the first time—in Eau Clair. Came to my door like flesh and blood, a little old woman this time. Maybe they aren't the same ... but they are—angels of death.... Death...." His voice dwindled away, his gaze at a distance. "Somehow I put her off. She came again to the woods late last fall."

"You saw her across the river today."

Slaughter nodded grimly. "It's been almost a year since Julia died."

Neither spoke for a time.

Out on the river nothing moved. The boss stared at the jammed stream. "Hell! We barely started and already we got a plug."

With explosives in saddlebags slung over his shoulders, Slaughter reached the head of the log jam two miles downstream. There was a bottleneck of three boulders concealed beneath the gorge of logs. Fourteen red shirted riverhogs worked along the perimeter of the jam, pulling, prying, lifting with their pike poles and iron hooked peavys.

Slaughter cleared them off the stream and positioned dynamite canisters, arranging the fusing back over the logs halfway to shore. He called for the all-clear, lit the fuses, then scrambled for the bank.

Suddenly far across the stream a riverhog hollered, waving his arms. Slaughter looked back and, seeing Jed still on the logs, jumped onto the jam, leaping from log to log upstream.

The charge exploded, casting an echoing boom down past the Chippewa. Great trunks catapulted into the air. The jam began to move. Water spouted up as timber fell. The pile relaxed, melting apart as the front logs shot downstream. The melt moved back upstream in a wave, quickly reaching Jedidiah where he walked the logs. He saw it coming and clambered toward shore. A free log whirled beneath his feet. He slipped. The log behind slammed forward crushing his calf and foot. Wriggling, he toppled and lost consciousness. A hand reached down, grabbing Jed out of the violent water. Ave Slaughter hoisted his nephew into his arms. Cleaving to a sailing log with his spikes, he turned to choose a path to shore.

The room in Eau Clair was quiet, but unconscious Jed still heard the river pealing through the sluice-gates of his mind.

"No, I've not come for the boy. I took him on the river. He's already mine."

Slaughter talked with the old lady not far from Jedidiah's bed. He looked over at the boy then back at her, demanding, "Is he gonna die?"

"You all die," she said, leaning on her cane. "Yet I am not death, but loss.

He stared at her wattled features and she looked back. Then slowly Slaughter began to see: *He* was the something for which she'd been willing to wait. The slow-coming for Jedidiah with its fear, enmeshing nights, and petulant gut. The awful pressure of fearing the loss of Jed.

His shoulders slumped and he turned away.

In the quiet, the floor creaked and he looked over at her. Her crooked back was turned; he knew she would vanish. But she glanced back over her shoulder. On her face a fierce light burned, purging her features like sunlight in the trees. For an instant she was strikingly transfigured and straight. Then she was gone.

Slaughter put his face to the wall, leaned into the crook of his arm and wept.

Jed was a hewer with splendid vigor; he swung his axe with pithy might. Around the woods sunrays dashed to earth, and youth's glad shout rang in the rhythmic swoop of his strokes. It resounded in the logging area up the banks of the Flambeau River.

He left off whacking at the red pine long enough to take a swig from the canteen his uncle handed him.

"Water's good and cold," he said. He equalized a stance between his real leg and the wooden one, and began throwing in his blade again.

Together the two men, one old, one young, watched the tree fall.

"You know," said Jed, looking about them at the woodland bristling with thin tall trunks. "It seems like a long time since white pine was great in the woods. Remember how big around those trunks were?—how tall they stood?"

Ave smiled slightly and nodded. He remembered.

The Magpie and the Ape

Herein is a Border Country tale on the origin of the English Wallflower. For it was in Olden Days that a lonely maid lived in an high Great Keep of the castle, at the behest of her father, the Earl of Tweed. His wife being dead, he feared for his daughter to be taken from him in marriage. Said daughter's visage was fair, her essential nature delicate as the flower's bloom, and to think of the loss of her maidenhead was more than he could bear. Wherefore, Avelina, as she was named, lived these three years up the winding stair at the top of The Keep, seldom visiting below. 'Twas as pleasant as a bower, with broidered hangings and a rosy fire in winter, and an huge black and white plumed magpie on the perch to make her company. But for all that, Avelina was more unhappy than the Earl's poorest thrall because she was a prisoner. Oft times she would stand at the window and stare down on the inner bailey were pages and maidservants trod; or mayhap she would sit on her stool embroidering a beast, creeping thing, or saint upon the Bishop's damask cope; then, at whiles, she might converse with the magpie. Yet oft would she lie upon her featherbed and weep.

Now the magpie knew that work best loved casteth a spell on the worker thereof. For the Bird took note on how that whene'er Avelina would sit embroidering, the tears would cease, her white brow clear, and peace rest upon her countenance. So one day, when it saw her staring sadly out the window, the magpie spoke. ~ Come hither my young lady and set thee to thy work. See how the head of the serpent wants fastening beneath the Lord Crist's holy foot. But the maiden moved not. ~ Nay Magpie, I cannot set it there. Canst not? returned the Bird. Avelina answered, 'Tis not meet for one to put beneath Crist's foot what one clutcheth to the bosom. Tush! said the Bird. What better place for it? But why saith thou hast an adder to thy pure bosom? Thou art not evil! Yet the maid protested, saying, had I not come to this prison, I would have thought not. But now 'tis revealed: I harbor this snake of self will; I grow bitter in confinement, yea, even against God.

Then she hung her head and wept. Whereupon the magpie clucked consolingly. Thence, scattering feathers, it flew to the shutter. Now this Crow was wonderful and that not for its speech, but because 'twas magic! It perched on the shutter and studied Avelina's faced with its dusky eye, the great black beak turning this way and that. Then with not a word, the Bird soared from The Keep. It circled the castle far above, seeing all going to and fro in the baileys below. But ever and anon, its gaze returned to the white-gold speck that was the face and hair of a lonely maid, fast in the hole of the tower. Thence, flapping its wings once more, the Bird embarked on a compass of the Earl's thralldom, and beyond, seeing the face of another with its inward eye.

Over the greensward, past River Tweed, beyond the wooded hill lay a neighboring estate. In a stout little fortalice abode White William, young and leal. For want of payment to the Duke he was denied a place in Baronage. In times past there was a feud over one piece of land betwixt William's father, Baron Harold Whitefoot, and Avelina's father, the Earl of Tweed. Without said land and its tolls, which the Earl now withheld from the Whitefoots, young William could not afford to buy his title. Whereas, once upon a time, William did romp about the Earl's palace on his knees as little Avelina's steed, he had since been banished for reason of the feud. His father was now dead and he had never seen Avelina in her woman's beauty dight.

On this spring day, William sat with his knights and the friar in the halle of his fortalice, planning war. Without the window, the fair day waned toward even. Tender green buds grew on brown twigs of the wych-elm, and the breeze was dainty. Of a sudden a great black bird appeared nigh the unshuttered opening. At once a solemnness descended, and the company, for a moment, was hushed (though all at unawares). And quietly William spake: Having challenged my father's once leal friend, I am of a sudden troubled with second thoughts. Sir

Robert cried out in vexation, This vengeance hast thou prepared ere thy manhood! Shalt thou give it over now? But William passed into gloom and made no answer. At length the friar said to the knights, We had better take our leave. And he thought, Mayhap this cloud will pass upon the morrow. But as the friar rose to go, lo! His eyes beheld the bird which was perched on the sill. ~ What is this!? cried he. Hast thou a pet, William? Peering up, William's eye lighted on the crow. ~ Nay, I have not. ~ Wottest thou whence it hails? ~ I wot said the young noble, rising from the board. He approached said Magpie desirous to study it, but as he looked a vision clung upon his eyes, to wit: he saw himself a lad, straddled in play by a golden child. Dimly, behind them perched a magpie. The scene changed ere the vision departed, and he beheld the maiden form of Avelina languishing in prison. All his anguish stirred and his brow was knit in toil. Anon the vision fled, and with it the bird. White William then bestirred himself; remembering that saying abroad that the Earl's daughter was held in a keep. He said right quick, Fellows stay awhile; stay I beg. And he clomb out the window, leaving his vassals to look after.

He hearkened first after the magpie, whither it went. Finding it not, he trod up and down the greensward gathering his thoughts and seeking wisdom. Hidden from view, the crow cleaved to a branch of the wych-elm watching William at his labor. Thinking William's earnest needed of reward, therefore, the magpie opened a store of cunning plots, imparting one to him. Eftsoons the young man's countenance lightened, and he smiled. Returning to his companions thence, the ringing of cups prevailed; for he renewed his pledge to war.

Meanwhile, the Earl and his pet, the Barbary Ape who conversed with him by signs, clomb the winding stair of the great stone Keep to visit his daughter. He bore a brace of thrushes, covered with a dainty sauce of almonds, spices and wine, on a silver platter. He drew the bolt and entered, whereupon the yellow monkey commenced frolicking about the chamber screaming and showing its yellow teeth. At length it settled in the rafters. ~ Daughter, quoth the Earl, I bring thee tidings of war. And she, uprist from the stool, said, What. Hast thou thrown down the gauntlet? ~ Nay. I have been challenged by young William Whitefoot, that ungrateful whelp! He shall dree the weird! ~ White William! cried Avelina. My beloved erstwhile playmate.... ~ Fie, daughter. Call not that one beloved. Quoth she as one dreaming, staring at the floor, I have not beheld his visage, low, these many years. ~ Neither shalt thou hence, warned the Earl. Instead shalt thou behold preparations below in the baileys where we stockpile for his siege (should he so haply such achieve). Ere he come a smith will climb to fasten a bolt inside yonder door. When we be in the throes of battle, thou shall make use of it to keep the alien knights without. At these words, the Ape screamed and stomped upon the beam with gleeful rapidity. Suzerain, thou fool! Thou art not comic but unseemly with thine antics. Behave lest I ship thee back to The Rock whence thou camest. His speech notwithstanding, the Earl grinned fondly on the hairy yellow beast.

Just then a fluttering of wings drave their attention to the window. The magpie lighted there, following its mission to White William's meager estate. The monkey, sore vexed at the bird's presence, increased its clamor to begin swinging about the room screaming at the magpie. The crow clucked and trod to and fro on the sill, saying, *maag maag maag*. ~ Ah, spake The Earl, the twain chaffer one with another. Suzerain, becalm thine uproarious bowels ere I thrust thee from the window. ~ Meantime upon seeing him, the Magpie had covertly cast a spell upon The Earl, for next he said, Daughter, I know that thy confinement burdeneth thee somewhat. Come to the halle with me on the morrow. We shall feast upon the dais and have our merriment whilst the men and maids do fortify the Castle. My villeins and knights shall come hither (but I shall take care that none come nigh thee.) We may make good cheer ere we be tried of that scoundrel. The Earl spake again to the yellow ape: Go to thou ape and descend to the halle with me for meat. ~ Then Avelina, upon her stool, heard the dropping of the bolt as it echoed down the keep, and the sound of her father conversing with that ape as they quitted the tower for life below.

Night passed and daybreak beamed across the Earl's thralldom, ushering wayfarers over the vast estate. These obtained entrance one by one of the porter, and the company within the fortress waxed great. Stores wert laid by; straw bundles spread to cushion missiles; forges were litten. The war engines rumbled as oxen drew them to emplacement along the walls.

Late in that day, The Earl, all clothed in furs and silks with a chaplet of red stones upon his brow, clomb the stairs with the Barbary Ape and loosed the bolt. When the door wast opened, the monkey and crow began again to spar. The Earl threatened the twain, but to no avail. ~ Daughter, I fear we must needs leave the Magpie in this place, lest they destroy the feast. So 'twas that Magpie stayed behind. The three began to descend, and on the stair the Earl promised Avelina that a company of minstrels wast bidden to the feast. ~ But fear not, for there be no miscreants, nor spies among them. The porter hath seen to that. Then he did but lightly pat her hand.

Within the palace halle, the boards across their trestles lay. The table upon the dais wast linen covered, and full of delights. To wit: roasts of venison, partridge, peacock, kid, and braces of diverse poultry, each in a dainty sauce; fruits, both dried and stewed in wine; frogs, snails, and eels; breads, cheeses, flagons of wine and ale; then liquorice to make sweet the breath. About the halle stood knights and ladies, squires and maids at boards with their trenchers, meat, and cups. There, too, fought the curs for bones among the rushes on the floor, and the Earl's pets caroused (apes, falcons, hounds, cats, and a young winged dragon or two). Thus their hearts wert merry made on the eve of war.

On the dais with the nobles, at the Earl's right hand, wast that yellow haired ape, eating fruits and leaves. Avelina, comely in her white lace gown, sat quietly in a canopied chair on the left hand of her father.

The imprisonment had deepened her to set her apart from this frivolity. Indeed, her separation wast now inwardly wrought, so that she had no fellowship with these at all (and the magpie wast not here for her company). Afterwards jolly minstrels came forth, praying all good weal upon the host and guests of honor with the raising of cups. Thence these brought forth the pipes and lutes, and musick filled the halle. The masked harlequin appeared for his pantomime; and he proved grotesque beyond imagining. His form wast sore misshapen with an hideous huge hump upon his back, and he could but hobble about almost on all fours. In dueling his wooden sword went a-thrusting, missing his opponent in ever waxing buffoonery, until the laughter rang about the halle. At last, in defeat upon the floor he croaked, Likewise shall William Whitefoot fight, and end, if he continue in his folly!! O how the company roared!

Howsoever, not of laughter rose in the maiden. The spectacle saddened and made her careful. Her hand was laid upon The Earl's doublet's sleeve. ~ Father, may I take my leave? His head the Earl inclined. ~ Art thou tired, little one? ~ Yea, verily. She stood, and the Earl beckoned for a matron, but the harlequin came forth and croaked, I pray thee my Lord, if I have pleased thee with my jest, I beg, let me escort The Lady. Her I'll safely speed to yon tower. ~ Upon my word! laughed The Earl. For thine apt performance, thou shalt have that favor. But see she speak to no man upon the way, thou ill-favored creature, thou.

The twain went thither in the darkness. The Harlequin, hobbling beside the maiden, took note on how that she withdrew herself somewhat from him. Asked he, Canst thou not abide one who is misshapen, Mistress? The maid stayed her, then said, in all quietness, 'Tis not thy form, but thine erstwhile mockery I disapprove. ~ Did not the Harlequin thee entertain as he did the others? ~ Nay, thou didst not. At this the Harlequin seemed to walk a whit taller. Answer truly then, saith he, Hast thou any feeling for that fellow William? Avelina glanced on him, fearing lest he be a spy. But she sighed, and turned her face towards The Keep. But low she said, I recall sweet fellowship from days gone by. How he was my dearest playmate, and fairest to behold. And her voice faltered as she spake those words, dearest and fairest. ~ The Harlequin started. At last he said, Dost thou know what manner of man he be? ~ Yea, if my judgment is trusty. He is like yonder star in the firmament: all white and true; beyond my reach. With wonderment the Harlequin swung his face up toward the black vault of heaven.

Forsooth he was White William, and now his heart did bang. ~ Fair Avelina, spake he softly, his voice no longer coarse. Fast her look was fixed on him. The knot upon his back was sore pronounced. He fumbled at it, hearkening to see if anyone was on the watch. Then, as she looked, he began to draw a cord of flax from out his hunch. Long it waxed, and he did twist it in a coil, speaking ever low. ~ Sweetling, I am William, and do now declare my love for thee. If thou lovest me, plight it now, for I have a plan whereby we may be wed.

Now fair Avelina wondered: could this selfsame ugly lump be her beloved? Howsoever, she knew it on the instant, and touched him tenderly with fingers all atremble. Yea, I plight my troth. Now they approached The Keep, the guard of which was fast asleep owing to a potion the Harlequin had covertly given him beforehand. William mounted up the ladder and entered that small door, and the maid forsook the starry night and clomb after. Up the winding stair they went, hand in hand, while their hearts beat sore. As they clomb, William spake in a voice both low and strong. My heart panteth after thee as deer do for the water brooks, and my troth shall be to thee alone. Such sweet sayings bestirred an answering in the maid. At length they reach the top and entered Avelina's chamber, all aglow with wax light. The magpie was nowhere to be seen. William hid the flaxen coil beneath the canopied bed. Then quoth he, Thou shalt make sure thine escape through the window. Fasten the cord about the timber, which thou mayst reach by drawing hither yonder chest. Thou must await my signal; to wit: When the siege tower doth overflow with men in battle, then shalt thou descend. I will straightway come for thee.

Heretofore the pair had been holding hands. Now William asked, Will thou grant me thy sweet kiss in token of our pledge? ~ Avelina answered softly, yea, if thou wilt show me how. Whereupon, still wearing his harlequin's mask, he embraced her and gently touched her lips with his. Then William fain would lie with her, but she, though all aroused, said, Lord, stay thy caresses dear. My maidenhead is thine as the marriage gift to thee. I pray, let all these sweet secrets remain until I am thine in name and heart, for then who shall gainsay it? ~ William answered, Beloved, thou art the bride without blemish, thou art wise in the bargain. He murmured, Sweetling we shall hold. He turned and strode quickly from the room, looking back but once upon her visage fair. He bethought himself to bolt the door, as had the guard done had he not slumbered. Only after the door was closed, and William's footsteps died, had Avelina any thought on how, for his mask, she had yet to see his face.

Meanwhile, nor maid nor man had taken note of that shadowy form, mutely grinning, among the rafters o'er the stair. When once the man took leave of the tower, this creature stirred. Long its reach in swinging down, descending toward the ladder. Thence the ape, traversing o'er the courtyard, was suddenly hailed from above. ~ Whither goest, hairy mite, in such haste? The monkey started then in fright and loathing. It screamed and hurried on its way, yet not ere Magpie flew at him. Now these two were a match in wizardry: The yellow beast with sorcerous power of coercion o'er unsuspecting fools, and the magpie somewhat of white power, developed in self will, the which she used to arrange things to her liking. So in magic, neither might suppress the other to gain mastery. Therefore, the bird used her talons on the primate, seizing the long talking fingers of his hands to crush them. He cried and writhed in torment. The men-at-arms ran to part them, but Magpie simply mounted on the wing and vanished into night.

When presented to The Earl, the monkey cried aloud, but the noble could make but nought of it, for Suzerain's fingers wert a bloody tangle. Hence, his treacherous mission was carried out in vain. The Earl did coddle his pet, and called for steeped herbs and poultices for its fingers. He would fain have ordered Magpie's execution, had it not been for his daughter's want of company in her doom.

Now proceed we to The Times of Battle betwixt William Whitefoot and the Earl of Tweed. Wreaths of smoke do arise from the Outer Bailey of the Castle, for The Earl was not forewarned of William's missiles of Greek fire; which do light among the straw cushions, catching all afire. Meanwhile, The Earl's men, from hoards upon the walls, pour boiling oil and molten lead on any foe who chance beneath. Arrows, both from the yew and armor-piercing crossbow, let fly through the early morning air. But underground, William and certain of his villeins wert privily finishing a tunnel which had been some months in the digging. Whilst William hit with pickaxe underground, he spake low beneath his breath, saying, Thou art comely as a coppice of sweet chestnuts, oak, or ash. The smell of thy garment is like forest at the dawning. Such things quoth he whilst the sweat rolled from off his back, and thoughts of Avelina rode his mind like stallions.

When then the hewing and digging were now finished, and the pillar set in place beneath the outer wall, William covered all in rendered fat and lit it with a torch. And once out upon the greensward, he watched as now The Wall fell in the pit, shaking the ground with thunderings. How William's men did roar! The ground shook beneath the war horses as they wert ridden to the breach. Armour glinting, swords and battle axes cleaving, heads a-flying, men sundered one another in the Outer Bailey of the Castle.

'Twas beyond the curtain wall of the inner bailey, high up in the keep, that tender hearted Avelina saw with horror and palpitations.

Betimes she flung herself upon her knees and prayed aloud. Howbeit she hearkened not to that crumbling mortar, clinking down the chimney. At sight of the siege tower moving slowly through the breach, she hasted to draw forth the chest beneath the crossbeam. How her heart banged as she fashioned up the knot. Of a sudden, accusation in full measure smote her: Wast she not betrayer of her father's trust? She stayed nigh the opening, dressed all in a green gallooned gown and bright yellow bonnet. There the revelation grew: The Earl did not trust her, for he had her in a prison. Now she wast becalmed, her inner person coming forth. At that moment, the siege tower spilled its men right o'er the curtain wall. Avelina clomb out on the sill, parlous high. The wind blew, but she blenched not as she cast the chord down the dizzy heights. Now Magpie fluttered past from going to and fro amongst the battlers, helping William's cause. The bird watched as, all green and yellow comely as spring, Avelina began now to descend.

Yonder, across the courtyard in helm and hauberk clad, William saw the green gown billow in the wind. He doffed his helm and stayed to see the blossom of his heart in her jeopardy, before starting towards the tower. But as she held, the chord let loose. The flower dropped: his heart stood still. How the echo of William's lament mingleth with the roar of young man at his war! And fallow his blade fell clattering down. 'Twas then a foe smote from behind, and, swiftly swinging with his mace, he broke William's skull.

Now, Magpie, circling up above, was witness to what passed. Swooping low she sought the man amongst the dead, but lo! he wast not. She flew then to the tower, seeking there the broken body of her mistress, when lo! there was nonesuch. Howsoever, there grew a green stemmed yellow flower, dight with veins of red; known thereafter as The Wallflower. And the there, too, grew a fair white clump of that flower named Sweet William.

Thence Magpie hearkened to a scream and, looking up, beheld Suzerain the Ape, swinging on the shutter. She wist that he had loosed the chord with his prehensile feet. Sadly taking to the wing, Magpie clomb above the tumult smoking. If thou'd look after, thou'dst see her belly white, and hear her on her way a'crying, *maaaag maaaag maaaag*.

The Comet of 1577

Jack Lewis, in night clothes and tamping a pipe, climbs a starlit knoll outside a sixteenth century Germanic village. Despite this attire, he wears walking shoes to avoid slipping on the frosty pasturage. As he approaches the crown he sees a white smoke-wreathed head, then the white figure emerging in its ascent of the opposite side. He recognizes Samuel Clemens immediately. They greet one another at the top of the knoll, shaking hands and exclaiming a bit over the conjunction. The astronomical term is fitting, given the setting of their fanciful but fortuitous encounter: two bodies on the mediaeval celestial sphere gaining the same longitude.

"Now let me guess," says Twain. "The year is 1577 and you've come out to observe the advent of a comet ushering us from our Aristotelian arrogance ... in order to surprise us out of the erroneous belief that all was fixed to its appropriate round beyond the planets. ...Are you researching for some book or lecture, or is it the poetry? But you've aged some since we last talked. Perhaps poetry is not quite the thing now?"

Lewis smiles. "Perhaps not."

They stand on the knoll together looking up through the crystalline spheres of the heavens above the river Glems, while, at a distance beneath, a woman and child climb towards them from a lane along a curve of Glems' stream. Even from here they can see that the child wears hosen and a cape, the woman mantled to her feet and wearing a white wimple with pillbox hat. But the comet is now visible above the mountain behind them and the men turn in silence and awe to give it their full attention. For long they watch as the quiet stream of light beams into view over the serrated silhouette of trees across the way, its self-possessed spirit of silence invoking the same in them.

At length they sense mother and child drawing near, but Twain speaks. "That cracking sound you hear up there is not just frost splitting those trees across that ridge. It is the sound of the solid spheres breaking up between the planets."

"Yes," murmurs Lewis, "Kepler, and Tycho Brahe with his instruments, observations and calculations, will see to that. Before long the cold and the dead, the dark and the void—empty of the music of Jove, of Venus and Saturn—will sweep in to clear the imagination of its bright celestially classical model. The high and sweet or even the pestilential influences of the planets will cease except where the zodiacal superstition persists.... But here are Kepler and his mother approaching. We shall overhear if we do not leave this place."

"Let's stay a minute anyway. We will only overhear in fancy, and what good is it to be tellers of tales if we neglect a found opportunity?"

The approaching pair were yet a little below the hilltop and speaking German, but each man heard enough of it in the clear cold night to understand that they were listening to familial woes. They supposed that the comet was blocked by the hill, not yet in view to these two mediaevals who had come to witness its presence in their lives.

"Then papa is not to be hanged?" piped the child's voice over the stillness of the slope.

"No, but we will be selling the house. He wants a tavern."

Having heard these words, the two men stepped away and were at Uraniborg on the Scarlet Island of Venus (Hveen). Here was the towered and turreted observatory of the Danish nobleman Tycho Brahe, parts of which were yet under construction. It was late. Moony silver gleamed faintly upon quadrants of some domes. One of the windows above was aglow with the light of the astronomer working out his meticulous schedule of observations for the comet of 1577.

They stood on a corner of the below-ground-level observatory beside the domed edifice of its main watchtower, this white figure of the 19st century and this dark one of the 20th. They watched quietly as two assistants positioned an elegant geometrically fashioned 5-foot triangular sextant of Tycho's design. Here also were domes under construction but low to the ground, for the astronomer would protect his instruments from inclement elements.

"What workmanship, elegant craftsmanship, they cared so much to perform," murmured Jack Lewis. "How well they worked," he said. "Where once beauty permeated everything they contrived to do, we've replaced this quality with quantity—valuing obsolescence as an economic essential. But in making well we were once able to work united with Beauty—not so attainable today, even if we can come out on a night like this to meet her merely as spectators. See how intent they are to be united not just with learning but with its beauty. They inquire into the things of created heaven with their carefully calibrated instruments. Of course, even in their sometimes exquisite theological considerations, they come near to missing it all—for the very source of what such images stand for *can* be missed, even in this sublime pursuit. Kepler, that sore sickly lad we saw, will be so yearning to have in his hands such elegant instruments, and run his gaze along such compilations of observations. Yet, somehow, one does not doubt his foundational value."

"I take your word on it," said Twain. "I haven't read him enough to know ... but maybe I shall study him by and by." The white figure beside Lewis drew upon his dark cigar.

It kindled, even as he stretched out his arm, the cigar yet between his fore finger and his thumb.

In that instant it was broad day, and the carts upon the street were already moving along with their wares or fodder. Both the humble and the delicately dressed were everywhere about their business, and there were shops and some hovels on either hand. In fact, as Lewis looked, he saw that now they stood *inside* one such hovel, filled with filth, and a prisoner—dirty, sore, and dejected in a corner with some shattered straw. The odor here was fetid, filled with pestilence and putrefaction.

"This is a tenant of the noble and meticulously exacting astronomer," said Twain. "As carefully, even lovingly, as he handles all his instruments and charts, you will find he so abuses his 'dependents'—stealing their goods for his own use—who must work like slaves—virtually are slaves. Not that you do not see profoundly similar abuses, and greatly multiplied, among the people in the 20st and 21st centuries, where, I'll grant, your beauty of construction and craftsmanship is sometimes seldom seen. And so much of that, as here, is supported and nourished by inhabitants of church."

"The 21st? Will I make it that far? Of course any amount of beautiful, dedicated and applied science would not right what even an elegant theology has not manage to obliterate in us....You know," said Lewis, "this is eerily like being in *The Mysterious Stranger* with your young 'angelic' antagonist, Satan."

"Oh you've been reading that, have you? I guess they published it after all, despite my daughter Clara's wishes. My dear Livy wouldn't hear of its being published, and I myself was never satisfied even in its completion. The story seems to melt part way through.... You know a book can get tired and sometimes does not want to finish itself properly. But the young Angel nearly convinced me by the time I was through."

"I *was* reading it just before coming out to seek Tycho's comet this evening. You've converted the Angels to determinism—? And then to nihilism?"

"The man who's a pessimist before age 48 knows too much. If he's an optimist after that he knows too little. Look at this... this—pathetic suffering—juxtaposed with such splendor. Wouldn't you say it is a nightmare?"

Lewis was silent. Then he said, "But you did not even let your protagonist Theodor awaken from it. Not really. Can you call a long life of tormenting turns followed by a nasty jolt and release into nothingness an awakening? A vague, pathetic, drifting thought—was that what your angel called him? And what, by the way, can a *nothing* hear to be disturbed by it? You may be right about the story's lack of structural success... or especially even philosophic success—Can you imagine nothingness enough to portray it? I can't." And he had to smile before continuing.

"But you are right to regard life as a kind of nightmare. I should think awakening from it would be more like having a scab fall from a healed wound. Theodor—excellent name!—spends his life moving from being a young innocent believer to one who is continually striving to patch up or shore up his flagging faith in the face of a very diabolic onslaught. In the end Satan has converted him to nihilism, by overwhelming him with the world's vast insupportable injustice, and then vanishes in a puff of having never existed. Now of course I did not think this quite fair of the angelic young nephew of Satan, but it was fitting, in character. The whole thing is very like Job with Job ending by cursing God, as his wife tempts him to do. Some men and women simply cannot stand the facade of false pieties, or even a more innocent but ignorant failure to doubt in the face of great evil. Many are quite comfortable to see its existence and never allow it to challenge them. But those who can't stand the comfortable for that may be the more savory. Yet since you do end with his believing in unbelief—this undeviating trajectory toward a kind of negative unity—maybe it's not such an unsuccessful story after all. I'm still not sure that given his characteristic quality of persevering innocence and belief Theodor would accept this."

As the allusion to historic suffering faded from around them and they found themselves on a starry road in Austria, Twain said dryly, "It lost its narrative arc about halfway through, I judge."

Sphere Flyer

Hidden in a dark crevice on scree slopes of the Antarctic Peninsula, a skipjack is about to hatch. His mother stands back on webbed toes, making room for his large rocking egg. A hooked bill, almost as long as hers, breaks through the shell. Chipping away, it stops and starts, this black tube-like bill. Moments later a sopping chick breaks free.

In early days of shipping, these birds were colloquially known by various names, and one of these was skipjack. A dusky Wilson's storm petrel, the small mother preens this newcomer and, although ravenous, she settles down over him to brood. Three days have passed since her mate took his turn brooding.

Suddenly comes fluttering wings and a short *coo* outside the rocky tunnel in the scree. Her mate has come.

The new father flounders to her through a narrow dim tunnel leading to the outside world. The female emits her soft short peep. She cocks her head to receive her mate's offering of partly digested shrimp. Then she steps awkwardly off the newly hatched storm petrel, plucks up some bits of shell and disappears up the narrow dark tunnel.

The male regurgitates still more musky-smelling crustacean down his offspring's gullet. He covers the new chick with his own warm body, tucks his head beneath a wing and promptly sleeps.

One day the chick is left alone longer than usual. Listening for their return, he hears thunder—of hundreds of thousands, a multitude of wings beating overhead outside the tunnel. Now all is profoundly silent.

He waits and waits for mother or father to come down through the dark. He nests in the darkness of these rocks, dozing and waking. This skipjack has never even seen the sky, nor flight of flocks. And he is so fat he can't get up the tunnel.

Troubled and uneasy, he sends lonely-sounding peeps into cramped darkness. But by the fifth day, his forced fast has diminished the body fat. He scrambles around in the crevice. A fierce storm passes overhead, sending whistling drafts down-tunnel to chill his slender fledgling body.

The storm beats. He trembles beneath the scree. Then the blizzard passes off and in its wake come curious sounds, muted coos, chuckles, squeaks. At last he is slim and eager enough to travel up the tunnel.

On uncertain webbed toes he makes his ungainly way up the crevice, then popping his dusky head through the snow covering. The vast world is startling blue and white! Blue sky above snowy slopes teems with low-flying brown squabs—all newly slim and fledged, all storm petrels. The air is broadcast with eerie soft calls, *pittirels* of sound.

The skipjack tumbles forward, and joyously opens his wings in first flight. Now the sky is home. He may not touch land again until returning with his mate many months from now. But how will they be guided over the great sphere of the world to the northern migratory waters?

The skipjack flickers in and out among these young storm petrels. He looks upon the frigid blue Weddell Sea and glides hungrily toward it.

Passing over the ice shelf, he spies a south polar skua hanging in air. Its pale body glistens beneath dark wings, proud head raised on a neck of golden hackles. A helpless white snow petrol is nipped in its beak. The skipjack banks off.

He dips to the water, trying the surface. He flutters up and drops back; hovering, dipping his tube-bill to snatch his very first live shrimp. In waters of -10°, he discovers dining airborne. The skipjack makes pass after pass until his belly is finally full.

All about him thousands of storm petrels are swarming, feeding. Among these young flying flocks, he cruises above the circumpolar ocean. Days begin dividing in periods of twilight and brief darkness. The untried flocks move northward, reading the sun as they go. Night becomes defined. A first magnitude star rises and sets. With large sensitive eyes, the birds begin flying beneath a moving map of heavenly light.

These flocks approach the thunderous Antarctic-Atlantic convergence. Below them lie abundant krill beds where four blue baleen whales dive, or troll the mountainous rolling surface. The skipjack flits across great waves, tipping his black bill for his share. Looking into green depths he sees one great sperm whale wrestling a giant squid.

Something flutters off his right wing. Pattering his feet along the deep trough, he sees the female storm petrel. He has seen this one before. She hovers barely an inch above the trough, wings a-quiver, her square tail fanned. He sees her dip and pick up a morsel then, hopping, she bounds up a sea-green wave. He follows.

Seeing him over her back, she flings her head, ridding her nostrils of saltwater. A stinging drop lands in the corner of his eye. He blinks his nictitating membrane, a transparent eyelid, to flush it out. "*Pit pit pit*," he cries, and gives up the chase.

Far off the vanished coast of South America, these fledged flocks move northward. They are pelagic—seabirds—shunning the coast whose magnetic fields they sense.

The skipjack flock follows a Mediterranean bound merchantman for a whole morning, clouds scudding above them. Brisk winds warn of a coming hurricane. Other followers of the smoking merchant ship include gull-sized sooty shearwaters. They have followed the great circle route around *Tierra del Fuego* from southern Pacific waters in order to spend the boreal summer in the North Atlantic. Soaring and diving, their wings shear steep waves as they pick up garbage spilled from the ship's galley. But the most powerful companions have fifteen-foot wingspans: three dazzling albatrosses looming through air.

Two men in sou'westers stand at a taffrail on the poop deck. Says Bearded about the albatrosses, "They looks like great ghosts, the way they follows after. See how graceful their feet folds under?"

"Aye," agrees the mate. "But now look a'yonder at that little birdie, aflying here." He points to the dusky but white-rumped skipjack, who flutters up from a trough with something nipped in its beak. "That's a Mother Carey's chicken, that is. Called so on account o'how it gets on in the storm. The Holy Mother looks out for'em, or so they say."

Bearded answers, "I saw one a'hanging in a sailing master's bunk once. Little thing had a wick down its throat and was blazing away for a lamp. They got some kind'o oil in their stomachs, flammable 'tis."

The men look at the sky. The seas grow steeper.

An hour later the storm extends full winds. Rains batter down. The merchantman blunders up on chaotic seas.

Dipping in and out among leaden-colored, white-foaming seas, the skipjack loses sight of this ship. He tosses on the winds, moth-like, until dark. He patters on the sea like a dancer, scarcely able to fly. When he is wearied, winds and rains hammer him into the seas. Again and again he pops up, wings pumping, regaining flight. Day and night it thunders, calming for hours, to refrain again in fury.

Then the storm wanes, leaving the storm petrel to glide out from under—hungry, beaten, used.

Exhausted, he picks up a meal, and another, soon settling down to snooze on calmer seas. He feels a fluttering, looks over to see the bedraggled female, settling to rest close beside. Together the storm birds sleep.

Together they fly many nights with warm equatorial air currents. The alabaster stars guide these two birds into the vicinity of Ascension Island.

They crest a current above off-island islets. Below them green turtles swim westward toward Brazil. These have left hatchery sands after depositing eggs. Many birds are in the air, mewing gulls and white fragile-looking fairy terns. Northward, a river of red flows between the sides of the sea. Hungry blue whales spout and play, crashing on waves. The two storm birds float down to feast on rich red plankton.

But as they descend something flashes above, a harsh cry startling them. Long-tailed *Jaeger*, thrice a skipjack's size, swoops down to take him. The petrel beats back, his scapular muscles straining. Wings splayed, pulse rushing, he wheels in the sky.

From above his mate shoots a reddish oily stream into the attacker's face. The skipjack follows suit. They spout a sticky substance over the Jaeger's eyes and crown. The enemy beats back. "*Kreeah*!!" He screams, banking in the opposite direction, flying away.

Trembling, the storm petrels drop down to the wavy red strip of ocean. The *Jaeger* is forgotten as they feed.

Cloud cover drifts across warm waters, dimming the sun's hot rays. As day passes, fully-fledged flocks reunite and begin moving into misty night-dark seas. Peeping and cooing, they call to one another. In the fog there are no star-lights for direction. They fly in circles or rest on the waves, in danger of being snatched by some hungry predator from below. Days become thick with overcast, but their northward urge persists.

Then, one night Skipjack awakens, blinking at the light of a second magnitude star. Twinkling above the ocean horizon, the star neither rises nor sets.

It brings these flocks to life. Their wings beat a sound of rejoicing as they take off toward the new star.

But each night the skipjack sees the star higher. As they approach northward, it shines stronger. *Polaris* of the North has become their guide. A bright asterism, the Big Dipper, rises and sets around it. *Ursa Minor* revolves around this hinging center. *All* stars and constellations have this pivotal point for their ordering.

With the star's aid, they will hop waves thousands of miles toward iceberg waters—toward Labrador and Ireland, towards perimeters of the Arctic. They fly the earth's sphere to the North, were seals and caribou migrate in spring. The oceanic Earth is always on the move. Its creatures go here and there.

Blue Runways

After long delays, two good flights—one for photos, the other to lift the night restriction from Allen's license. The first flight was around 6:00 p.m., in the Cessna 152. As we sat waiting to back-taxi for takeoff from the Auburn airport, I watched the traffic, heavier than usual. One poor landing: a small Cessna stalled too high above the runway—bounced hard, almost flipped. He taxied to the ramp and I thought him finished for the day. The Emotional Gamut of Flight.

Before takeoff the usual jitters. But, as we mounted into the north, I caught sight of our Cessna-shaped shadow going over ground below us, limned in shimmering gold fire. The lowering sun, beaming a full mellow light gave our shadow the saint's halo I've written about in these pages before. Swiftly as we rose it lost its plane shape, becoming a diffuse bright spot and following in parallel with us across the easterly landscape. Both its initial and changing appearance were owing to our changing position relative to the sun.

Before liftoff I had seen that the "poor-landing man" had not given up for the day. He back-taxied out and took off directly behind us. Looking back at the now tiny runway, I was anxious when I couldn't locate him. Was he below us? Allen said maybe he banked away to make another practice approach.

All the land spread before us in evening light, shadowy and golden. Great cloud shadows lay silently upon undulant Maine greenness. One could sense their silence even in a noisy craft.

We were on our way to photograph from above the Washburn-Norlands Living History Center and the new heirloom orchards—for illustrations to adorn the apple booklet written in Tansy Town last summer. We had no charts but the Androscoggin to lead us; for the Norlands, where my apple subjects had lived in the nineteenth century, lay northward between the river and Route 4. I had other landmarks in mind as well—three principal ponds in Livermore

Township. Bartlett Pond would be especially telltale, curving around the foot of the Norlands hill.

Now Auburn Lake, on our left, reflected the sun at a shallow angle, sheening the water. Almost directly below snaked the black, motionless Androscoggin, very wide at this point. Dr. ElizabethWood, in her Science For the Airplane Passenger, explains that reflection angles correspond to the angle at which light enters the water body—the old "angle of incidence equals the angle of reflection" law. Why couldn't the river catch the same sheen as that when we came up from Auburn Lake? Because of my position overhead, the viewing angle was too steep to intercept the low reflecting angle. Had I been east of the river I'd have seen the reflection.

The look of the world changes by virtue of my position. It changes by virtue of the atmosphere and the apparent position of the sun. Artists learn this changing of perspective with their constant attitude of observation. The variableness of appearances would be more disconcerting if it weren't for the fact that we're used to it and constantly learning. In a habit of observation, researchers learn immutable laws through mutable appearances.

Allen and I flew on, searching out and finding many orchards—sweet orderly lines in an irregular patternless land. We could approach the Norlands simply by heading north, but the landscape was so vast, its forms and farms so numerous, that I feared we would miss our goal. I had forgotten to keep primary landmarks in mind, remembering only that if we came to Livermore Falls we'd gone too far. Just then I spied the white Norlands steeple in the midst of green land. A surge of pointed joy rushed up in me. And there was Bartlett's pond, curving at the foot of the hill.

The tiny dear buildings grew, glowing steadily in the evening light. The Norlands house glowed as though molten white gold. Its surrounding grounds shone with every shade of green.

Something was happening in me. An emotional affection expanded in my being, even as the little barn, church and house grew larger . . .because of this heavenly perspective. The sense of duty, so often felt while working on the booklet, dropped away to earth where it belonged. Norlands was the brightest thing in creation. The Washburns, whom I had researched in letters, old journals and musty account books; whose very lives I had indexed: All were exceedingly dear. I was looking down on their handiwork and place of experience, realizing for the first time that it yet contained some of their spirit.

Excited now, I wound and clicked, wound and clicked off shots with Allen's old yard sale Yashica Twinflex, He circled as I shot, then headed back for the airport. But, in leaving the Norlands behind we flew toward Bear Mountain, evocative landform, which the Washburns appreciated viewing from their porch in all weathers. It stood before us immense—monolithic—as we bobbed along like an insect. A great dim pluton lit from behind by hallowing haze. The combination of position, atmosphere, and sinking sunlight revealed Bear as a pluton of the underworld arisen, and profoundly whole. Learning and imagination play their ultimate role of revelation.

Now, in passing the mountain, I flew the plane, taking the controls longer than I had on the Wiscasset flight; feeling my sense of the medium increase but slightly. Am able now joyously (or recklessly?) to assume the skills of pilot as I do those skills of an artist; sensing similarity in the learning process. Maybe one necessity is the basic underlying belief, born of past experience, that I might conceivably learn what I may choose. I want to feel the craft roll at my touch, turn to the pressure of my feet. Am surprised by the thought that I might learn to fly. My hands and feet, my gut and the seat of my pants know so little now. My mind easily forgets technical things that it has absorbed from talk and print. Yet one day I may land some craft right down there on that thin runway, placed just so in Auburn, Maine. (Where, according to Allen's instructor Chuck, British pilots learned to fly Spitfires for World War II.)

Allen was now on base-leg, heading for final approach, and my ears were popping. The vain personal dream was quickly replaced by the personal fear of landing. Looking out the window: There was our round shadow, haloed, and, descending, I focused all my attention upon it. It grew to the shape of a Cessna, rushing toward landing alongside us, expanding to the size of our earth-coming craft. As I watched, its wheels reached to meet our own. We met in touching earth, a Cessna and its shadow, and no more limned in light.

Its shape changed. Taxiing, the shadow on this concrete was no longer plane-shaped but chunky and squat. Long rays of evening's light, coupled with its place regained on the earth, had turned it comical, misshapen.

I notice the poor-landing pilot and his young family—a wife and toddler on a bench near the runway. He is excited, talking to his little one about watching Daddy fly the plane. He leaves and walks back to the craft. The young wife seems bewildered, apprehensive, forlorn. Something in me recognizes this scene; the eagerness of the student for his subject, the quiet dejection of the related onlooker, holding on to her little charge lest he wander onto the busy ramp.

It's after 8:00 p.m. when we meet Chuck at the Piper Warrior for a checkout flight, and to lift the night restriction from Allen's license. On take off the Warrior proves a dream craft, stable and smooth flying. Unlike the Cessna, it is a low winged plane with lots of visibility above and outward. . . if more limited below.

It is dusk as we rise from Auburn's low hills. Streaks of light in the west make purple bands of the clouds, stretching from north to south. A splotch of deep red marks the sun's place. Mountains of the north and west rise slowly and fully on the horizon, but now they are hushed in a rosy dusk. We turn on a white wing, the opposite wing rising high against the red light.

Shooting a few touch-and-go's. The mountains sinking, range by range, disappear as we drop toward the runway. We touch, we rise, we go. Bank on a wing, do it again. I have no problem with this. The Warrior is safely a dream, and I am easy inside. There comes a final touch and we go.

Now all the land lies in a deepening blue hush. Behind, Lewiston glitters like Christmas flung across deep earth. The Casco Bay appears, a dim blue-gray, still holding some light. Portland: tiny gems strung along a faint horizon, melding with sea/sky. As we approach from above, coastal towns become lines of light, spreading back and outward.

Allen, in front of me at the controls, is pleased with the Warrior. He holds his hands out for me to see: the craft is trimmed for straight and level flight; it holds its configuration without drift.

The world beneath is sleeping in magic. Have myself been at peace since we began. Oh, soul is wonderfully easy in this, and could go on and on. On our right Sebago Lake, deepest of Maine's lakes, is lightened blue. Casco Bay on the left is a dull expanse. Would like to see more of Portland's lights as we approach, but am too low, down behind the pilots. I look out the window at islands in the Bay, looking like tufts of dark moss. So at peace, I will gladly take what sights I'm offered.

We bank, turn. Now below is rich with lights. Back Cove is ringed with lights, almost a circle. The jewels of Portland are strewn below.

Chuck has set the radio frequency. It crackles. "Runway one eight, cleared for touch-and-go."

As we draw near on base-leg, I see detailing of dim houses, lit by the glow of jewels. We sink. Comes the light-trimmed runway. The dual blue necklaces of the taxiway passing. We touch, slacken . . . . Now a burst of throttle—the thrusting transition from touch to go. We rise on that assertive power, we go and go.

The painted lady below, Old Orchard Beach: a resort of the Québécois. Its regular lights are lined like necklaces on the gaudy bosom of the shore. Biddeford-Saco: a maze of sunken light on the edge of Maine's rural darkness: The old textile town, partly comprised of decrepit old mills. Flying toward Sanford. The lit precision of the turnpike, moving line of light, cutting through black velvet.

Lifting my eyes toward the weather, the smog, a dark mist to the south: The lights of Massachusetts, extension of the great American megalopolis, are shrouded in this misty darkness. But the Maine corridor (so-called by geographers, statisticians, demographers) really shows up while flying at night. It is that strip of Maine—running from the southwest corner of Kittery up into Central Maine at Bangor—in which population is densest. It is an extension of the great Northeast corridor, known as Bos-Wash. This is where business is transacted, industry and commerce and government. Here policy is set, the lives of God's creatures impinged upon. And here the state's transportation network is concentrated. Yet, for all that, the corridor contains lakes, waterways, resorts and even most of the state's farms—with extensions along the coast, and in one corner of Aroostook. The remainder of Maine sleeps in darkness and trees.

Businesslike squawk of air traffic voices. A constant stream of clipped communication. No fumbled words, coughs, or hesitation. Short, precise, yet arcane. Myriad numbers and weird words signifying the abstract—tango sierra zulu golf.

I touch Allen on the shoulder to point out blipping traffic—light at one o'clock, at our altitude, headed for us. The Portland controller mentions "unidentified aircraft" heading our way.

Chuck plays with the radio, picking up commercial stations on the other bands. It bursts loud, obnoxious. He turns a headphoned lurid face at me, which, in the red panel light, throws him completely out of character. I grimace and look away. The radio grates out a garbled warning about invading visitors. It's only a commercial, I remind myself, but stress and imagination connect it with the approaching traffic. The winking light crosses above, moving off westward, after the vanished sun.

Relieved, I look for stars while keeping an intermittent watch for more traffic. But stars are faint and few. My flashlight for note-taking goes dim. I'm fatigued. My initial peace, the peace of the Auburn sunset, is gone. Was it real?

Our altitude seems shallow. Lights are scattered sparsely, dimly below. They look pale, blue, worth little. It takes forever to cross dim Sebago. Lakes are less dark and rimed with scarce ghostly light. Land between lakes and lights is dark as asphalt. Gratefully, I see at last the little "Lewy" runway lights straight ahead. The Portland controller asks if we have them in view.

Allen shoots an ILS approach. The Instrument Landing System is comprised of a glide path and azimuth radio signal. Intercepting them, he aligns precisely with the runway, slides down as though on a shoot. Instruments are mysterious marvels, but securing.

Back once again in the air-school office lobby, Chuck talks about depth perception with Allen. He says that at night one's depth perception is inaccurate. It becomes a hazard to safe landing.

Illusions and misleading physical sensations are often experienced during flight. Their sources can be varied: G-force, fatigue, turbulence, lack of oxygen, inner ear, etc . . . . Then there's vertigo—all one's being obliterated by darkness and cloud where there is no direction known. These are reasons why flight instruments are so important. When one's own sense fails or misleads, the instruments are there to be believed.

Vijaya and the Seven Hundred Find Lanka

Vijaya was rolling on the sea with seven hundred of his followers in seven sickle-shaped, hemp-bound reed ships. Vijaya was a Sinhalese prince, the son of Sinhabahu who had the paws of a lion for hands and feet because he was the son of Sinhala the lion. Vijaya was half-shaven; the right side of his head had been shaved by his father as a sign of disgrace. The ocean wind lifted the long dark remains of his hair, swirling them about his face. The sea was white-capped and deep, and Vijaya leaned on a bamboo rail staring unhappily at the water.

He and the Seven Hundred had been turned out to sea from Gujarat many months before in order to placate the wrath of his father's subjects. The unruly behavior and violent play of the prince and his male followers had disrupted the kingdom. Vijaya wondered at his father's intolerance and hypocrisy, for Sinhabahu had also been violent in his youth. In fact, he had slain his own father, the lion Sinhalal Yet remember-ance of this had not been enough to help him ignore the demands of his people.

"Send the prince away reproached!" Their clangor still rang in Vijaya's ears, causing him to wince even now.

Just then his captain Sena came over to him carrying a brass ladle full of water. Sena's head (like those of all the Seven Hundred) was also half-shaven, and he worse his remaining hair in a plait that trailed over his shoulder.

His black eyes showed concern* "Trouble roils your spirit. Prince."

Overhead the changing wind smacked the square-rigged cotton sail, flapping it. After some moments, Vijaya answered, "I can't forget my humiliation."

Holding out the dipper of fresh water, Sena urged, "Sleep can abate grief. If you'll let it, the rocking ocean will lull your hurt."

Vijaya waved aside water and suggestion, and went astern to row. Relieving another of the long oar, he reclined on a grass mat in the curve of the stern, falling into sculling rhythm beside the young noble Gopura.

Bright was the day they found Lanka. The hot coppery sands stained red the hands of Vijaya and the Seven Hundred as they fell, «xh»u«t»d, to •hore. They made camp at the edge of the woods at Tambapanni where the sun stood over the high dim forest of palms.

Following his meal of lasuna peppered rice and fish, Vijaya heaved a contented sigh and etood. The silken air and scent of the land had given him relief from his Brief, renewing his will.

"Come, Sena, let's walk."

They tramped a mile through the woods befoi halting at a blue lake. Between the arms of the woods a flock of white pelicans, sailing low, fished the waters, to one side ebony and satinwood trees lined a hidden lagoon, which they entered. Conclaves of egrets nested there. And on the shoals fat dry crocodiles, jaws agape* sunned themselves and waited.

"This is truly a Resplendent Land," murmured Vijaya.

"What, Prince?" asked Sena, breaking from his own reverie.

"This place, Sena, shall be called Lanka henceforth. Here, if we can overcome its dangers, we shall start life anew."

They returned slowly to camp. As they drew near, the god Upulvan, hidden in the simple form of a wandering ascetic, approached them through the trees.

The little ascetic bowed humbly and took up Vijaya's wrists. He held them together palm to palm and wound the hands with khoroa thread. "I bind your hands to strengthen you in temptation. How you are sealed against is as long as you will." The seeming ascetic looked up at him and smiled. In his smile was a sparkling well from which the spirit of Vijaya drank thirstily. Then the ascetic vanished and so did the thread, yet Vijaya felt its binding still.

"Did you see that. Sena7?!" He turned to his friend.

But juat then a skinny dun-colored bitch came bounding through the spindly palm trunks.

"Look. Leader. A pariah!"

By now some of the other followers, having seen them returning, came close to look at the dog.. , „

"This means civilization is near. someone shouted.

And another suggested, "Let's follow the dog and see where it leadsl"

"No doubt to the house of a noble!" exclaimed yet a third.

But Vijaya sensed something amiss and said firmly that they should not go after it.

So all returned to iheir camps except Mitta. who went following after the bitch. Through Lanka he went over limestone and bog(over deadfall and stream he sprang. Hot a sign of humanity did he see. Mile after mile he followed the dog until presently it began to bay.

Deep in the forest there was a glen where Kuveni the sorceress sat under a banyan tree, spinning. She smiled faintly when she heard the cry of the returning dog. Both dog and Kuveni were demons in disguise. They planned .to destroy Vijaya and eat the Seven Hundred.

The animal shot between the down-growing branches of the banyan and lighted on a great crystal of quartz, grinning.

Mitta loped into the glen and beheld the sight of Kuveni the beautiful, spinning koseyya and singing. A pond sat silent beside the tree. Silken thread trailing from the distaff gleamed prettily in the afternoon light» and the damsel smiled at him. I'm lovely, come, she seemed to invite. Spellbound, Mitta proceeded.

When he came close, Kuveni rose swiftly in anger for she recognized the god Upulvan's seal already on him because he was under Vijaya's authority. Therefore she could not yet devour him. Rapacious fires roared in her eyes as she seized him by the throat and threw him into the chasm beneath the waters of the pond. Down he sank without a cry.

Kuveni straightened her sari and glared at the bitch who took off through the banyan branches to gather more men. Then the seeming woman sank back against the thick yellow-green trunk, muttering against Upulvan.

The pariah returned to the camps, this time luring Kula the huntsman away.

Thus, one by one, six hundred and ninety-nine went astray from the commandment of Vijaya, until only Gopura—whose name means gate-tower—was left with him. Together they watched Sena disappear between the king coconuts.

"So...Gopura. Only you and I are left while the others go, day and night, to find what they may. What is it they want that causes them to follow a bitch instead of me?" But he understood the weakness of their flesh.

"I am true to my name," boasted Gopura. "Though Sena and all the others go. I won't, Leader."

"We'll see," said Vijaya.

It was night when Vijaya threw a crimson kambala around his shoulders for warmth, and, leaving the fire, started off through the seasonal forest in search of his seven hundred compatriots. His dignity was gracefully expressed as he traveled noiselessly through the dark strange web-work of Lanka. Only the small and wakeful great-eyed loris noted his passing.

Meanwhile, Kuveni had an abyss full of paralyzed .men but needed one more—the sum\of all—in order to break apart the protection of Upulvan and eat them. She sat in the opalescent night trusting the dog to return with Vijaya. Kuveni begrudged sharing the men with the other demon so she occupied her moments in thinking how to do the dog out of its meal.

When the pariah crossed Vijaya's path he followed her to the glen. Entering there he took in the sight: the grinning dog, Kuveni spinning, the moon in the pool. The woman was desirable, but the approach to the water was thoroughly trampled. Wondering who she was, Vijaya tried the spirit of the smiling woman against that of the wandering ascetic, and found it specious.

Taking his hesitation as an evil sign, she jumped up. But he sprang to the offense, taking her by the hair. Winding his fist in the tresses he pressed upon her skull. Thus the seal of Upulvan upon his hands prevented her spirit from exiting its temporary abode.

"Spit up my men, witch, lest I send you where you would not go."

Kuveni yielded to the prince's straightened will, saying coldly to the dog, "Go, bitch! let the water out of my sink."

With its tail 'twixt its legs, the dog descended a hole between the roots of the banyan tree, returning not again. Moments later the water in the pool began draining with great suction to reveal bodies piled to the rim of the chasm. Kuveni uttered a few words in the fore-tongue of Chinflulays. Immediately the men on top. Sena and Gopura among them revived and clambered out. Each successive layer followed, with the men at the bottom taking footholds in the rock fissures and tree roots to reach the berm. At last Mitta stood on the bank beside the empty pond.

One by one they approached the prince and kissed his free hand in gratitude very pleasing to witness.

Vtjaya sternly reproved the sorceress and admonished her to repent.

"Can a demon repent?" she asked, where up» the puzzled prince released her hair. She vanished.

Between the glen and the sea, the wild aniroais of Lanka woke and scattered before the great return of Vijaya and the Seven Hundred.

The Balker

"Enos Chupp is the man to redeem Kugelblitz," thought Hans, as they pulled into the lot beside the sale barn which sat, white and sprawling, off the the edge of the race track behind the farriers at the fair. This training of his horse for Hans was happening after some Amish had begun moving into Quakertown.

Hans led Mule through the barn opening and into the stall that he had reserved for the red standard bred. The barn smelled of pungent fresh manure.

Hans wiped Mule down with a piece of old blanket, and patted the colt. "It will soon be over, little one, and then you will be a better horse. An animal of worth and use." He walked away.

As a rule's Mule didn't care for humans, but Hans, at least, with someone who stood out among them. The sorrel shifted his eyes and blinked at the footsteps echoed into the distance.

Moments later he realized he was alone. In the corner stall he heard the jumping and sucking of a "cribber." Arching his neck, he saw the black ears and unmarked forehead of another, a hairless horse. Gulping down air, she made wet sucking noises while clamping her teeth on the wooden stall rail. The horse had begun to assimilate stress into her nature. The habit she had acquired which reduced or prevented her usefulness had caused her owner to neglect her. Parasitic and unkempt, she whiled away her empty hours chewing wood and swallowing air.

Hans had come back and was noticing all this. He thought, this would almost certainly be Kugelblitz's fate if Enos Chupp failed to break him of balking.

~~~~~~~~~~~~~~~~~~~~~

Enos Chupp sat at a wooden banister on the edge of a platform behind the small Freiburg arena, explaining his methods in a twangy
~~~~~~~~~~~~~~~~~~~~~

Midwestern tongue. In a semi circle before him was the 15-foot-wide sawdust covered arena where he would demonstrate expertise with problem horses. Beyond, rows of folding chairs rose in tiers were a few farmers and knots of Amishmen sat. Fresh-looking little boys and Amish youths with dangling Salem cigarettes and Louis L'Amour westerns in their back pockets gazed down on Chupp as he talked. Hans stood watching.

"If broken by brute force, an animal's bad habits will remain, making him incompletely trained and a nuisance to his owner. Out west a man might break his mount with spurs, a bullwhip, maybe a mouthful'a curses and it'll take a month before the horse's even rideable. He'll wind up with a four-legged package of bad habits. There is easier ways'a doin' things." Chupp put up a wrinkle hand, spotted with age, and smoothed his long yellow-white beard.

"Yessir. It takes patient repetition, kindness, and firm resolve to get out of your animal results whereby you can respect him and have satisfaction. Applying this technique you can gain the compliance of a wild horse in a single day."

The audience noted astonishment. Hans had heard something about this.

He leaned over the wooden banister and spat into the sawdust. Next he turned to Hans, who stood by the door left of the semicircular demonstration area. "Have you got a sound horse ready for me?"

Hans nodded and opened the spring-tie door. He ushered Mule into the arena.

"He's a stargazer," Chupp remarked to the audience. "Holds his head to high for practicality. You must teach the horse that you are master. Your object is to bring the animal to submission. What's this colt's shortcoming?" He asked Hans.

"He's a balker, sir."

Chupp picked up the animal's near side front hoof, massaging the cannon, ankle, and pastern, reassuring Mule that a man's touch need not harm him. With smooth moves, Chupp wrapped a hemp foot-strap around each pastern just above the hoof. Although Mule didn't care for this he permitted the man, whom he trusted, this liberty.

A 20-foot longe line was threaded through rings on the surcingle and snapped to the near side front foot-strap. Now Mule had all the trappings of Fetters and was yet somewhat disposed toward the man.

But the kind hands and friendly form disappeared.

Suddenly, from behind, Mule's new acquaintance commanded him to "giddyap."

But this was not a command Mule obeyed.

The man yanked the pastern rope taut, putting the sorrel's leg up, tumbling him forward. Mule reared angrily.

"Giddyap!" yelled the man, smacking a whip on Mule's farside buttock. On three legs the colt tottered forward and stopped.

Hans stood by twisting his suspender, watching.

"Giddyap!" Once more the whip stung Mule's rump. His anger submerged into humility as, thus hampered, he scrambled wildly toward the locker door at the opposite end of the semi-circle.

"Take away his leg and you take down his high opinion of himself" said Enos Chupp to the audience. He walked around the horse, grabbed the hackamore, and pulled him off the door to face the people. Again and again he drove Mule up and down the length of the demonstration area. Each time the the horse obeyed he was praised. Next Chupp reached down and threaded the rope through a ring on the farside pastern strap, Hans watched grimly.

Yelling "giddyap". again Chupp drove Mule forward. But this time bewildered Mule found himself falling, deprived of both front legs. Frantically he reared high into the air, neighing wildly. Struggling, snorting, he tried regaining the legs, but to no avail. The man had taken his mighty legs and would not release them. He crashed to his knees in shame. His young owner winced at this humiliation,

Chupp turned to caution the audience to do this type of training on sod or sawdust to prevent injury. "We don't want him hurt. We want only to rid him of conceit so that he will obey."

With that he released slack on Mule's farside fetter, allowing the heavily breathing beast to rise shakily on three feet.

"Giddyap!"

Mule leapt. /

"Whoa" But Mule kept going.

"Whoa, I say!" And yanking swiftly the man took Mule's far front leg. Screaming, he reared and tumbled again. He lay breathing arrhythttrically, his cannons and fetlocks tied up with his forearms.

Hans looked away, disquieted.

Chupp talked to the audience, the line still taut in his powerful hands. "Never, never, never use 'whoa' to slow your horse.Use 'whoa' only to stop. him. Otherwise you confuse him."

He laid his head on the horse's heaving sweaty barrel, fanning his own face with his hat. Looking up at Hans, he invited the young Amish man to take his turn with Kugelblitz.

Hans glanced into the older man's face and saw a kindly expression seated there. The young man's disquiet at seeing his horse thus treated was transformed into poignancy. A love for Kugelblitz he had never felt before, emerged. With a sense of awe he took the longe line.

What gratification as the sorrel moved to fulfill his command!

It was dusk as Kugelblitz trotted home to his bucket of oats, drawing a box buggy,its occupant, and the Morgan behind. The air was soft in his nostrils, his strength felt good. Hans was thinking, when life's difficulties are done are done enjoyment of the little things is enhanced.

Lost Nation

Meantime, somewhere among the folds of the Grandmaster's garments, 'twas Anna Damini 1521, the past of a parallel universe. Someday (in this land of the alternate universe) would be condominiums, malls, an Olympic Village with industrial works underground. In a suburb just west of the great city of HiTopOLis, but a scant league past the neighborhood of SiXPointz, in A.D. 1521, 'twas a camp of the Ehio—the Eihoerrian, or Caht People.

In a cave in the rock half-a-league from the encampment lived a friar. Here great ice had disappeared leaving massive rocks abut, stones older than what underlay as bedrock. In a cave, not damp, nor full of badgers and worms, was the friar's stone cell with books and manuscripts in wooden racks. Though small, made of twigs and slender, these racks were tied together with deerskin thongs, sturdily. Other furnishings he had: deer-tallow candles alight on the rock floor by his knees, a small stone hearth with embers glowing, surmounted with rough-split oak mantelpiece. On this mantle two small earthen bowls held fragrant herbs and conifer smoldering, mingling with the friar's upsending prayers.

Father Domino knelt in ragged homespun on a mat of cornstalks woven by his own hands during winter, sometimes in the cell, but often sitting with believing native brothers and sisters outside in the bright Elios-light when weather proved mild. He had lived with the Caht People (as some knew them) long enough to convert but a score to the faith, and these had all become neighbors and friends by virtue of his mild manners and quiet smile; and because he taught them strange but believable things.

His chanting was quiet, almost a whisper, sometimes a humming, or wistful thrumming in his chest; almost never heard outside the cave. "Raison d'être, Raison d'être." His friends rarely heard but knew he was in here—behind thickets, in summer hiding an entrance which, in winter, was hung in deer hide to shield from cold. Father Domino had decided soon to take down these skins draping antlers wedged in the rocks. He would need to make a skin garment now his robe was rags, and the bugs of spring to be biting.

He paused, and stood to take out a precious hand-copied codex, opening to a particular spot. All in this, the Next World, was hand-made. The revolution in machine-making, of which some of his books ere made, was not yet among these A'ndyans, natives of the Next World. Letters here in this book were lit, some, as with gilt fire. While he scanned them, candlelight leapt over the glistening mica-stone walls, reflecting on the page. It glittered also across his now upraised and dreaming eyes. No one was there to see it, no one to hear him murmur, no one to feel the salt water trickle down his tallow brown cheek and caress it—as did the spirit accompanying him.

"...A vesture dipped in blood...."

The words, of course, were spoken in Latinum, a translation of Grake made by himself before he came to the Ehio to witness these very truths to Caht People. The Caht People, whose cloaks were fringed with cat-tails, named themselves Ehioerrian, or People of the Lake and Other Waters.

He put back the book and gazed down at the embers, heedless of faint scents—conifer gently wafting a bit of smoke through the small cell. Up and out the smoke hole among rocks above the hearth, up and out went the smoke and too his breath, and the last of his prayer.

It must mean his own blood. Must it not? Must it not mean the blood of Raison d'être?

Thoughtful, he pushed back the curtain of gray deerskin and peered through the thicket beneath. Steep and high, the ledge above, and crowned in conifer, with others hardwood stems soon to unfurl. Tall trunks of oaks, walnuts, and maples stood against the rock, dark and wet, but as yet without leaves. These would come, in due course with spring showers, but latterly would follow summer thunderstorms, always short-lived and not unwelcome. For the Ehioerrian loved wild nature.

No one was without. Slowly he stepped through swollen red stems, droplets soaking his ragged shoulders, deerskin-and-thonged feet dampened in leaf mold of uncounted years. A little later he saw the family of Geagosasa moving down through morning mist beyond the thicket stems, down toward springs easing into the Little Ehio River, tributary to the Bigger—some miles below the land they all inhabited at present.

This present was a time of hiding. For all waited hidden, hoping for news of the truce. A truce was what they wanted with the Bird-Crested People, as they were known to the Ehio A'ndyans. These enemies knew them as Caht People for the many panther tails fringing their cloaks of deer or panther skin—taken from creatures in the hunt.

But this was the trouble, these cat skins and tails of the Caht People (or Nation du Chat in the tongue of Father Domino). The Bird-Crested People wanted the vain cat-killing stopped. But that was before-this-time, when the Caht People refused, saying all here belong to them for their use. The others, known to themselves as Haudenosuni, were a Confederate peoples and too many (in coalition) for Nation du Chat in battle. Now the Ehioerrian were to be destroyed, as promised, by the Bird-Crested People. Many battles had been fought with the Bird-Crested People, who lived eastward in mountains. They came and fought in these lands south of the Great Lake bearing Caht People's name. The Ehio had defeated that nation each time, but now more were coming, many more. Too many to kill in battle. But more, these enemies have thunder arms from strangers. The Haudenosuni vowed utterly to destroy them, take them in slavery, empty these lands of Ehio until the great cats should return.

"Geagosasa, ma dame," said the friar. Though chilled, he approached with such quiet almost to startle—had not this princess been used to such silent approach. As leader of the clan, this is what she was, to Father Domino—the princess. For the He-suit, being Frankish and Usi'opan, thought always of royalty and authority and how best to practice courtesy as a matter of course.

"Much Birdsong and sweet fern and goodness to you, and may Our Lady Mother and the Holy Father of Us All bless you, ma dame," said he.

Geagosasa had bent to pluck the pale green curled heads of bird-fern, sprouting from earth. Her rush pouch was rapidly filling. Down toward the tributary, her daughter Leaping Fawn also bent to damp earth for the spring harvest. Antipatihee, big brother, was with her, tall and lithely muscled. He was maybe eight-and-ten summers, and she but fourteen. Her black braid hung down to the ground as she stooped, and it trailed among spring spears of green, and the wet brown leaves plastered to earth by winter snows.

Geagosasa stood. Her black braid but threaded with silver-gray trailed down her bosom vested in doeskin. Soft 'twould be to the touch, but Father Domino had schooled himself not to notice these things. Geagosasa, as with all girls and women, were not made for the elements of his manhood, but for dieu. And for themselves and their husbands. Father Domino would not be ashamed on the last day.

First, she answered his blessing with one of her own. Then she said to the slender shivering friar, "You want to know of the treaty, jeune père. The friar looked younger than but was several summers the elder of Antipatihee.

"We have no word... as yet," she said. "The envoy is missing these several days since you went to study your signals."

She knew what he did in the cell behind thickets hid in the rock. She knew he had what he called holy letters, codes; like the signals etched in trees, sent up in smoke, or whistled forth — as if from one of the creatures (in warning or reply to other signals).

...But his skin signals were different....

She had seen the books and parchments from overseas, and how beautiful of pattern, and of elemental seriousness of purpose. The marks of his own making from his own dyes were not so beautiful, but she knew about their hidden message (hidden from her if not from Leaping Fawn). And that his marks were as important, almost, as those made so pleasantly shining and colorful by far older hands. Hands that, he had said, were now dust but leaving these wonderful signals behind. Others might now see the visions they conjured. Indeed, Geagosasa had seen these visions by words he spoke from them.

Everything here was dim with mist. They four—three natives and the friar—seemed alone in this land of making and breathing and slow-springings to life from the Maker Father Domino told of. She had no check to her learning of this, as had some of the Caht People. As soon as he told them, by the fire in the evening many moons ago—after he came in summer before—she knew on the instant 'twas true. There was a Greatest One. One to start everything. What she understood not was why all had not the impress to tell them 'twere so. The friar said it was so meant, but that neither she nor he might say why.

"Old Father," said Leaping Fawn, joining them, her girl's face with high cheekbones and black eyes animated. Her rush pouch was slung full on her arm. "Blackberry has had her babies. Five in all. You must come see them."

Geagosasa put her arm around her daughter's slender shoulders as they stood together.

"Blackberry, Blackberry... now let me see," said tall Antipatihee coming behind her. "It's bound to be either skunk or rat. Which is it, sister? Skunk or rat?"

"She happens to be raccoon, terrible brother. But if she were skunk or rat. What? They each are fine, too." She showed him smug eyes.

Together they went down, treading through tips of skunk cabbage, and twigs of sweet fern emerging with tiny leafbuds... down toward the Little Ehio River, its mumbling waters there in soft morning mist.

"Horn-in-Morning will return soon, will he not?" said Father Domino. He wanted peace seated within their spirits again.

Then Geagosasa frowned slightly. Gazing at her children, who watched her intently, she wondered what would happen to them in this land if the goodwill effort failed. "I will pray to the Father and Mother you speak of. Will you not?"

"Je l'ai fait," said he. "Toujours."

The one thing Father Domino sometimes misses here among the Nation is the scholarly community of his brothers northeast of the great lake. North of the Great Lake Ehio was a Brothery where missions met at whiles to share knowledge and books. Father Domino was always learning and desiring to share knowledge with others. However, some learning experiences were not congenial to him. Such as this now with young Leaping Fawn at the raccoon's den where, in this moment, the mother of kits slept as they suckled. Raccoons be nocturnal. The smell of the den into which the two peered was of musk, musty and full of crushed fir needles, rank beasts' smells. Here the two crouched together whispering nigh the rock crevice not far from his own, more comfortable, cave. In the same steep ledge of dark but, here and there, glimmering rock.

"See how her hands are almost like our hands, Old Father?" Leaping Fawn asked this without turning or raising her eyes to him. Delicately she lifted one of Blackberry's small paws.

He stooped a little behind her, for in truth he was afraid. It was a massive bitch coon. The raccoon, he doubted not, would not like him. She would not want him near nor even looking upon her and the kits. Leaping Fawn however was a friend (so to speak) of the family. She knew all the elder kits (femelles et les mâles) from the year before and all knew and accepted her.

Now the great furred beast breathed contentedly in her sleep—a mythical creature with its black-and-white mask, its pointed bewhiskered face and pert dark ears. Leaping Fawn was near, and no matter that other strange mannish scent.... All would be well. Some of the kits squirmed, and some lay sluggish, supine or prone beneath her. All masked eyes were closed. The musk smell was very strong. Later the friar would fill his cell with the odor of smoldering balsam. Then he would sit down and write all things learned of the girl and his own observations. That was what he liked most of all in this time and place—to be somewhat out of this present time, present place; and among the signs of the books and careful placement of knowledge.

On leaving these thickets beneath the steep-sided ledge—to walk more and talk more of what they had seen—and as they walked over deadfall and leaf mold and emerging white star and mayflowers, the friar said, "Leaping Fawn."

"Yes, Old Father."

"Leaping Fawn, I observed you swiftly climbing the eastern hillside the other night, away from the tributaries and up into heights beyond the rock ledge in which I dwell. There was, again, I saw, the quick ardor you showed once before when I looked. Forgive me...." And he thought, But having restrained my curiosity ere now, I wonder if you may sometime consider sharing your secret with me. For I doubt not you have some wonderful mystery to share.

"Old Father, I would say nothing now." Leaping Fawn evinced no sign of discomfort, as might one so young in another place and time.

"It may be, someday?"

"Mais oui. It may be."

Straight way he took up raccoons again. "Now you have, no doubt, a story for me concerning the good mother — or another of her kind?"

"Old Father, she is a wise woman because devoted to her kits. She shows them to wash their food, and where to den, feed, and how to be safe from enemies. She is a trickster because they learn tricks of her to survive. Upon one time she took off her mask and turned red like a fox to lead hunters astray. Man would be lead to her den but comes instead to the foxhole. He does not like to eat foxes."

"But how is he tricked? He is following what he thinks is a fox? Not liking fox flesh, why would he do this?"

"Aha. Because he thinks this fox is but trying to outwit him and so will lead him to the coon's den instead." Leaping Fawn smiled with relish and glee.

With a respectful nod, Father Domino smiled.

"You have given me much to think about today. And," with a gesture, "see how the land has lightened."

They had been looking in earnest on all roundabout them, for the leaving mist had shed shining droplets everywhere, on all twigs and buds — red and gold and green — clothing all with delicate enchantment. They walked on, speaking little but looking and smiling. And indeed they, both, were enchanted.

"What will you do with your bird-fern heads, you and your mother Geagosasa?"

"You, Old Father, must come and see. You must be very hungry after all that studying many signs."

The friar smiled, turning to her sweet exotic face with darkling eyes and fullness where her cheekbones just showed but would one day be prominent. "Ah, you know me well now, Mother Raccoon," said he.

She laughed like the murmuring of a swiftling brook, leaping and fleeting.

He pulled back the deerskin over the rock entrance and went once more into the cave. Now it was dark, candle- and ember-light gone. Then he took down the hide. Light filtered in and he gathered his inks, feather quills, and parchment. He had to write while Elios shone through budding thickets on his stone table, not far outside the cell. There was much to think of. Those hands, for instance. Yes, they were much like little hands, those raccoon paws.

He was inclined to agree with Brother Augusto in the manner of the Maker's revolving creation and recreation. The similarities, hand to paw, were by no means mere coincidence. All this was planned and set in motion to begin with. Indeed, sometimes he wondered (but to himself only and to the Great One who knew all his thoughts)—sometimes he wondered if there were no beginning and no ending. If all things revolved (as do planets around Elios), if all lost parts, and gained parts, and changed parts over time. Would this not fit with His Being in the midst, and with being both First and Last?

Then, as he set out his inks and lay open the paper-skin. He thought now instead about the great plague as had happened in Usia two hundred years ago. And how all that death had happened in the darkness of Usia, possibly because mice with disease-bearing lice had gone there from Usi'opa. So that Usia had but few folk.

Father Domino sometimes wondered what the world had been like if events great and small had not happened as they did.

He placed the cornstalk mat on the small square rock, and seated himself before the greater sandstone rock used for the table. He placed inks and quill-pen and parchment there. He shook down his ragged sleeves to begin writing.... But he paused his quill, gazing on sprouting life as it lined all twigs with delicate coloring, some reddish of various shades, some greenish. ...And here and there golden, like those beechen candle flames about to unfurl in the thickets. He put down his quill-pen and began then to worship with fervor.

No one watching might tell it except for, sometimes, the thrumming soft, deep inside. But no one watched. The encampment at half a league's distance would be busy now. True, the hunters would be about in parties after older bucks. Precautionary for the future needs of Nation du Chat, no yearlings would be sought. Only the great cats (for the Ehio's vanity) were not spared. Again, on finishing worship, he thought of the words. "...Wearing a vesture dipped in blood." And again he thought, Il doit signifier son propre sang (It must mean his own blood).

Now again he shook down his sleeves and began to write of the morning's findings. After, with ink and quill on a different parchment, he pursued his ongoing thought about plague aversion in Usi'opa, and how this may have changed the course of history over the face of the whole heavenly wanderer. If, for instance, the plague had not been averted by prayer a great loss of populace would certainly have delayed Madame Columba's discovery of the Next World — nearly 124 years ago in Anna Damini 1396. But then why, anyway, did it take so long as it did? Why did we not know about the Next World till lately? Ah yes. The Doctrine of Dryland had negated the theory of Other Worlds, that is, other lands in Eartha. All believed there was solely one land in a desert of ocean. There had been but the one continent in geological ages past; however the belief of but the one kept explorers from discovering the Next World far longer than need be. ...And, had it not been for lack of plague, certainly the "thunder arms," as Nation du Chat called them would not have so soon been invented; nor lens-glass, nor steam engines conceived (as he had heard of Brother Pinochio); nor clock works, etc. until long after these happened in fact. The slant-eyed orange people of Usia, he knew, were still very backward and sparse, and now a source of slave labor (till, as he hoped, the machines should free them). Surely 'twould not have been so had the lice and mice of Usi'opa not plagued, keeping Usia from being great. Now, also, it should not have been known among civilized peoples how the lice and the mice and the microbes made ill ... had Usi'opan medicine not so far advanced ... for that no plague. This, he thought, scratching the side of his nose with his quill (it needed a new dipping) — this would explain the robust colonization and the fabrication of things wonderful for the use of humankind.

Now. About the other.... Surely the Holy Mother in the Vanticantle of Roma would someday — may it be sooner than later — allow that making and remaking has filled the Cogmos.... Possibly there would be no brutal inquiries into these things — but only such as sane women and men might allow, meaning la curiosité intellectuelle — and all would certainly be well for learning, and for scholarship.

A swift fleeting rustling flicker among leaves at his feet made the friar leap onto the table, knocking askew and scattering his writing materials.

Il était là!! The Haudenosuni Moccasin! O deadly deadly! Deadly! And he had escaped just in time!

Oh, oh, oh. The Holy Father! Holy Mother! Oh holy ones thank you. Oh thank you, my holy friends.

But he knew not he had spoken aloud.

"Ma dame?"

"Oui, mon petit père?"

Among members of the clan, Geagosasa sat crosslegged on her mat eating coal-roasted bird-fern coils before a wide bed of ashes. All sat thus eating, happily so. Here were many families gathered to the feast of fern-heads, the children romping and feeding from mothers' and fathers' hands, or those of sisters and aunts. Elios struck down through budding mighty limbs with yellow light. Some folk sat on moldering deadfall, sometimes stirring ashes to seek out roasted fernheads.

The friar said, "We (in Franke) have a musical instrument part of which shape is like to this." Gingerly he picked out a coiled fern head and held it up for the others to see. "One plays on this instrument with a bow." He put the succulent coiled fern in his mouth, chewing and speaking around it. "Not the bow with arrows, but like this." The friar then pantomimed the play one does on the great upright fiddle.

"How sounds this music?" Geagosasa asked, head of the clan. She would they learned of the friar's strange place. "It is not like our jon-jon." She mimed beating the skin drumhead. "Is it like the bird-pipe?" She pretended the slender A'ndyan pipe.

Another nearby at the edge of the circle—a young man—picked such a pipe from his belt thong. He began vigorously to play.

All were happy, now at peace. The many men and women, the children playing, all were merry and forgetful of trouble. Horn-in-Morning and the envoy had returned with news of truce. No formal treaty had been crafted, but the promise was theirs that attack would not be imminent.

Only Leaping Fawn, the friar noticed, looked distant, withdrawn. And this was not usual for her. She was the first to make merry when it were decorous. Antipatihee, the friar saw, also noticed and fell silent. Geagosasa gave her daughter a coaxing look and spoke a few words to her.

Leaping Fawn took her gaze off the embers and pulled close her doeskin cloak with a shiver. She but glanced at her mother then back toward the embers. Sounding under the camp's merriment, tree frogs trilled in deep woodland. The stream below, murmuring, fell rippling out of sight under a leaf strewn bank.

Tumbling Beaver knocked into Leaping Fawn as he ran from his tormentor, little Broad-stroke. The girl grabbed Tumbling Beaver, fiercely, before he could glance away. Leaping Fawn hugged him and spoke softly into his ear. But he squirmed mightily. She let him go. Then he clung to her, giggling.

Afterward, as he went upstream toward his cell, Father Domino saw her fleeting through thickets, noiseless. In fact, he but saw with the corner of his eye. He turned. Yes, it was Leaping Fawn. The friar saw her start up the wooded hillside where below the streambed bent around and out of sight. She was fierce. Climbing with great ferocity and verve. He could not see her face, but judged it, too, was fierce... and perhaps unseeing. He thought she must be enthralled. But it was not her way, he knew. So then all he might do was wonder.

And, too, he now considered the awful request made of him back at the encampment.

She had come to him next day to explain.... Perhaps?

Watching him she said the two words with subtle emphasis. "You see Old Father, it's THE DEER." She said nothing more, and he waited. He did not rush her but looked up at the sky through gently leafing limbs and twigs. Soon woodland and encampment light would be dappled dusky green but now earth and trees and sky are open—all gently almost imperceptibly breathing.

She too waited, watching him look with his strange blue eyes at blue sky and twining deeps of tall trees above. She saw the fringe of his lashes and how beautiful he looked, Old Father.

To her mother Geagosasa he was jeune père, mon petit père, but to her Old Father. In ways he seemed old and she felt the oldness in him as from some old culture deeper than her own. To Leaping Fawn the Ehio were ever young. We have old stories but no one knows how old and, received, the stories also are ever young. 'Twas the depth of his knowledge, its variety and presentation making her feel him—very old. All ancient—old like the hidden roots of trees that showed only when one of these giants fell over with thundering and upheaval. Her own people might be displaced with little effort, small power, and they would be so displaced (she knew). But his people could but be thrown down—like the tree, with great power and calamity.

Tumbling Beaver came through the buds, swiping with his small self-made tomhawk, a stick and broken flint-head (discarded by his big brother) and tied with gut.

Voice strong and piping, he said, "I know about the deer! The deer is her friend!" He came up to them and continued apace. "He's like in stories. You can't see him with your eyes. Only in your story eye is he visible." Tumbling Beaver was not as slim as some of the children, but hefty and stolid; black of hair and eye as were the Ehio.

"And have you seen him there, Tumbling Beaver?" asked the friar.

"Only when Leaping Fawn tells me of him." He looked up at her, arms akimbo, the tomhawk in his fist pointed behind him. "Only if she tells me."

"I don't tell him," she said, looking at Father Domino.

"Once she did. When we lay in the stream."

"Yes, once. But if you don't go away I can't tell Father Domino."

"Why?"

"Because too many looking at The Deer when I speak might keep him away."

Tumbling Beaver looked down at his tomhawk. "Then, I will go away... and let Old Father see him."

"Come." She opened her arms but he turned away, swiping. Walking through twigs. Then he turned back, as she knew he would, and hugged her as she bent to him. Now he looked solemnly up at both and walked off, much cheered.

"See," said the Father. "He repents and is better."

"Yes. That is a good of life. It comes from The Deer."

Gently he would correct, but thought better of it. He had her now. The deer. Kindly he said, "Tell me of your deer."

"He is not my deer. I am one of his People." She smiled softly, a challenge.

"I see." He brushed back his brown hair a moment with his fingertips.

"You should put that in a thong. Let me tie it back for you."

But he was embarrassed. She saw his face color. For a moment it grew almost as dark as Antipatihee's. She looked down at her clasped hands, sorry she had troubled him.

"You chase the deer? Is that it?"

"Not so much chasing as following after. But yesterday I chased him. He would not stay. I was troubled. Old Father?" She looked up at him.

"Please. More about the deer first?"

"Do you want him for your signals?"

"Signals? Oh, yes, signals. Yes for the words I am putting into parchments. There will be books of you all one day. And this is how we will have your stories to read in a faraway land. Not just my own land but others as well."

"Where the Franke live in great stone buildings, stone shaped as when we shape our awls, arrows and axes?"

"And others, many other, nations, lands. In many tongues the stories will be told."

"I must consider now," she said.

He bowed his head in acquiescence. The smell of simmon was deep here. He loved the sharp scent. He loved it.

"Old Father, will you tell me — though I have not told you yet what you want?"

"What is that, my child?" He took some care to use the formal more paternal term.

"Will you get the thunder arms—as they have asked you? As Horn-in-Morning asks?" Firm, she gazed at him.

"The Ehio will use them to kill their brother A'ndyans."

"That is no reason to them. They will ask you if the Franke use them on their brother enemies."

How shrewd is Leaping Fawn! He turned his face aside. Then up.

Again she saw his fringed blue eyes wide.

"I will have to tell them no," he said. He looked back at her. "Somehow."

He could not tell from her gaze, her solemn expression, what she thought of this.

"He said, "They don't need them, surely? Horn-in-Morning has a good report. Why does he ask me, I wonder."

She looked at him. "But you know, Old Father."

He nodded. "I know, young Leaping Fawn."

Heirolynn Out of the Gorge

The year was *Anno Domine* 1769, but the girl did not know it.

In the spring night at the stone-age encampment she fed sticks to the cook fire, one at a time. (The sticks had been gathered in woods along the river.) The fire caught well, flames stepping up the pile, shining into her eyes. She crept back beneath the deep-hanging rock-ledge, again to grind dried kernels into cornmeal with the grinding stone. But for reflecting fire it was dark night. It was A.D. 1769 but she did not know about Time. She did not know of time past. She did not know of time ahead.

Kneeling on cold hard rock she ground fine the maize she had planted, tended and dried—down by the rapids of the gorge where soil was rich and deep. There had been squash and beans, and a store of acorns, beechnuts, and dried berries she would yet be grinding for meal, with which to make cakes and pemmican. And there would be other provender for carrying away, roasted and dried. But she did not think of it. She used both her small hands and ground diligently upon the kernals with a cobblestone from the river. She was nine years old but she did not know it.

Her hands were different in hue from that of her captors, the *True People*. Her skin was the hue of the interlopers who must be kept away, lest there come too many for use by True People. As the girl herself was of use. She understood, rarely, that she was kept, in part, to keep the others away. Often this was forgotten. Hardly anything was remembered.

The Cat-people had been destroyed not far from here, not long ago—to the last child—but she did not know it. She did not know of the Cat-people, though she had heard mention of *People-from-the-Big-Hill* and *People-of-the-Great-Swamp*. Both were of that league of the Longhouse, *Haudenosaunee*. Those two peoples had utterly annihilated the *Lost Nation*, as the Cat-people would be known by interlopers in some future time. She did not know of future time.

She bent to the maize-meal, sifting it, sniffing it. She liked the meal scent. It reminded her of something good and kind. Good and kind were but elusive feelings without any words for them. She had been told nothing of the interlopers but that they be repelled. This was remembered sometimes. Sometimes she saw interlopers again, unexpectedly. She saw them in the same way as seeing what the medicine man or storyteller placed in her mind's eye. These speakers made things visible that had not been there a moment before. The newly visible people and things would be familiar in look by their recurrence in the story or telling. Interlopers looked different and the storytellers did not put them there for her to see. But they came of their own... and she loved them, yet also she was afraid.

The interlopers were cruelly treated, smote, laughed at for cowardice shining in their eyes. They were slain there before her gaze. Again and again. Stoned and cut and stomped. This had happened also to her, but she had not cried. So they kept her. But mostly she did not know this last part, this reason. She had forgotten it. But she saw the bleak turmoil of the slaughter again, heard again the shrieks and cries, seeing their tears shining, falling, before they went down around and on top of her, slain. The heavy bodies covered her and she looked up suddenly, gasping—

There was the fire now, ready with coals for the roasting, and baking of cakes.

True People were themselves dispossessed from the coastal plain by the interlopers. From there they had come away to the deep forest. Now, sparsely, they filled the place of the Cat-people in these wooded hills and valleys. Some of them, too, fringed their buckskin cloaks, as had the others, in cat's tails—the lynx, as the Fronche would call them. These were not now so numerous. The tails were harder to achieve. The girl had one of her own. She had taken this when no one noticed and kept it hidden in a crevice under the ledge. Sometimes she took it out and felt it all over, rubbed its softness gently along her cheek and the backs of her small thin hands. It reminded her.... She could almost see the face of the interloper it tried telling her of.... But not quite. No. She could not see. But sometimes, when she was sleeping, she saw the face bending over her, smiling and light. It did not look like the faces around her on waking. And she could never remember it after.

She looked over at Crowfeather sitting there in coal-light, crosslegged, sewing doeskin with sinew. No, the face would not look like that. Not high with bones, high with looks, not so dark as that. Not those black eyes, pulled straight at their corners.

They were talking now, as she laid cakes on hot stone prepared with oil of the green nut husks. Things seen came into her head as they spoke. These were men's voices but she did not think of that, she did not think which men's voices; though if she had they would turn out to be Clovenfoot and Eaglebeak. The pictures showed True People talking to the *Haudenosaunee* whose language-stock was different. *Haudenosaunee are not to do with True People as they did to the Cat-people*—said the Haudenosaunee with the hair that stood high on their heads, stiff like the crests of birds. They want to smoke the pipe and treat with True People to make war, joining together against interlopers. *So that is good*, say the things seen, full of sunlight and clouds, the top of the hill, the scent of the pipe. The interlopers will be destroyed and we will live and keep on in this place. We will not be driven from here as from that other place far away nigh the sea. And we will have weapons, the long slender sticks that flash and roar.

The slender sticks came into her mind. They were in hands held out, arms stretched and level, left arm crooked, covered in coat sleeves she had not seen before. But she had seen them before: She just did not remember. She did not remember the three-corner hats they wore, but she saw them. She gazed at the cakes among the coals without seeing the cakes.

These things are what I saw before, she thought now. But not in these words, not in words. *I have seen these men with tails under their hats. I have seen the sticks flaming.*

And they turned to her like that, smiling, and they called *Heirolynn*, and they ran after fallen game. But she could not see what game. She could not remember it. Their faces were pale, they went away.

Intently she lay studying the pattern above her, white stars snared amid high branches and crisscrossed twigs. Every-which-way, fascinating. She studied and found the precise weave of the pattern, warp and weft, and how each small bright white star so rightly fit in its twig-sewn space. The next time she looked, the stars had moved places, but that meant it was right to study again. Her bed was spruce covered in patched deerskin she herself had sewn of leftovers Crowfeather permitted by leaving them there for the girl to find. She fitted the feel of the spruce twigs beneath her into the pattern.

The rapids below sounded rough and white. True People were talking about her. It did not often happen. She was stupid and clumsy. One not far away in the woodland had said this against her. Said another beneath the pattern of stars and twigs, *But she did not cry.* Voices trading words in the dark and among white rough rapids sounding.

She can grind maize without stopping until done. See how she sets the twigs to make the fire? Just so. No one does that. And with great concentration. She stares but not in a good trance like the *meteu*. She doesn't look went I speak. She is an interloper. We can do some but not all to make her True People.

The talk fitted into the pattern she saw. Here it was: sounds in the surrounding, above-looking and below-feeling. It all aligned this way, that way: Just so. There. It was right now. All were perfectly fitted together. The girl fell down into sleep. She did not think it. It was part of a pattern, too, that she did not know she fell down into sleep.

In the next day's pattern she ground maize, and wandered away. The river was here, flowing on her left hand hanging loose by her side. Sometimes as she walked the hand flew up, the thin arm. She saw it from the corner of her eye. If she tried to do it, to see it fly up by looking directly, it went away. The flying part went away. She kept following downstream, away from the rapids. More Rapids would show, it was part of a pattern.

Not True People. Clumsy. Stupid.

The pattern picked up the song, sing-song. The girl's chanting continued, gathering bits and pieces of words, of syllables, sounds; the chippings of birds, the clickings of squirrels. If anyone came—the fixed look of the fawn. Everything went into the pattern of everything, and she passed by True People river bathers and kept on. They were calling to her and laughing, it fitted the pattern: The sing-song ceased before the calling started, it ceased at the fixed look of the fawn.

The girl drifted on going deeper and deeper, the gorge growing greater, the stream longer. On kept the girl, her arms sometimes flapping. Once she stopped to examine the rock. She climbed onto it, weathered and worn. Not smooth, not rough. Some texture between. Dark. It sloped. She sat down, her feet and legs dangling over the edge. Her palms were flat on the rock, either side of her. She looked at the grim rock, not at the view with twig patterns etching, surrounding brown hillsides. The rock grew older and older. She sensed this because the rock made her older and older. There was a long time ago, she saw briefly now. There was a very long time ago filled with strange things. There was ice, she heard the envoy saying; saw the great ice told him by the crest-headed people. Long, long ago. Long. Long. Long, long. Long-long ago-ago, long long ago. Before the interlopers, long long ago. Almost now she was the rock. The girl was the rock of long long ago.

The afternoon shone into the river ahead where the river stopped, walled with deep forest. She kept on toward it: over freshets falling, over deadfall, over springs gurgling, over rocks large and small, sometimes the arm flapping, sometimes it was still. There ahead the bright sunfall sheeted the river. On she kept, walls of the gorge parting. Yellow-golden light—pouring through there ahead—made the girl forget herself, the singsong of herself. Forget she was clumsy, stupid, not True People. Golden light lit with dust fetched her deep into a pattern, yellow-light-shaft ending the river ahead.

But now. As she went, abruptly the pattern changed. The sing-song stopping, quiet light pouring onto the river ... but the river was changed. It did *not* end. The river did not stop but kept going, looping, amid low green patches; there were oxbows. It turned a different way. She did not recollect names of the six directions so much as the pattern, new pattern itself speaking the old True People word. *South.* The river turned south around the lowering hillside.

" '*The ice!* " She sang it then, seeing it. " 'We will be as the great ice growing and pushing. We will push, together, interlopers away.' " Her thin voice, in the words of True People, sang upwards without thought out of the departing gorge.

The steep wooded hillside of the bend lowered away southward on the river's far side. Many times the clumsy girl had fallen on the journey down river.

It was dark before she stopped to lay down for the pattern. She lay on the hillside gazing into trees, gazing beyond to the moon-brightened dimming of stars. She did not see the moon directly. It was there in the hill behind, casting brightness. She did not see the clan planning the-getting-back-of-her to them, nor hear their words spoken in trees by the cook-fire beneath the great overhanging rock. Nor did she have pictures for her mind's eye that this would have conjured had she heard.

She studied the pattern, such as it was: There was the wider sky above the river, there the steep hillside, the river sinuous long sometimes looping beneath it. There, straight above, were the branches and small few faint stars. There the sounds of the wind—not down here with her. —The faint jolting beat almost dead center of her. She shivered and chattered and burrowed deeper. The leaves began covering her by her hands plucking them. The chattering stopped, the shivering. If she had but known it: She'd gone to sleep again in the pattern of life. A pattern of life's captivity.

Something woke her. She did not know what, nor care; did not think of it. The moon shone on her now, great calm white eye not in a pattern but in the sky. She jumped up, the leaves falling from her. She stood still. The sounds were none but an owl hooting, one remote over there, one up there; and of softly flowing river, down where the moon lapped in it. It shone there also, she saw, further down-river's length. She went low to the sandbar in its long curve and stood looking. Then she stooped and brought damp sand up, rubbed it on her arms, on her legs. She shivered and jumped. She knelt in the wet sand, leaned to the water, stuck in her face, waggled and washed it. She drank then the water, stood and walked down the stream in moonlight, going on. Going on.

Going on, going on. She did not now drift, not wander so much as look about at all things there for her gaze, moon showing shadows and twisting of roots and leafless bushes, deadfall and sandbars and curves. She liked the feel of the sand in her feet, the arches and soles, the gripping toes. She liked deep woodland soil with its blanket of leaves.

When she walked into dawn there joined the river with another making it more. Two Rivers, she saw, and the flight of geese overhead going back the way she had come. Dawn showed the tips of nearby twigs, swollen and reddish, where alders and willows tangled and hung in the flood two streams were making. She waded in and walked, she swam to the upstream out of the confluence and climbed out, dripping—as befitted the pattern—on the right hand side. Not the sun's side—the other side, the west, given the movements of light. Time was unknown. It was the movement of light on the work she did—work she'd stepped out of, stepped out of that pattern and into the river's pattern. Rivers moved different from light, but not from rain, not from snow, nor snow's several kinds. River was a fullness of these moving over the earth and in troughs, and hollows; quicker here, slower there. Rain fell most in sheets, but sometimes in pieces. So too did snow. But all fell. Light she did not perceive as falling except when it sometimes looked like a wall coming down from clouds, in broad strokes and very still.

The girl was walking upstream. One side of the ravine, on her left hand, was spread broad, not narrow as in the gorge where were the rapids, and the cooking cave that was high wide and cold. Above her it steepened on her right hand.

She did not fit the scouts in a pattern, coming downstream from the gorge in vessels, canoes. Not *True People*, not *Cat-people*, *interlopers*, bird-crest-people, swamp, hill—people, the kind she had had pictured for her in the mind's eye. People did not fit well the pattern. Most times they were beings unaccounted for, intruding, unwanted, requiring. The maize made sense, the grinding stone, the awl to poke holes for the pattern in deerskin. Now they were nought—the people were nought, even the familiar True People. She did not fit the scouts, coming after her, into the pattern.

The river's pattern she was working, her trail aligning, the leavings of her feet, their imprint stitching behind her. She looked back and saw them in a curve of the sandbar, following her. The other rivers were now behind, traveling northward while she traveled south. While the moon had shone the way, the first river had turned and twisted across and through a pattern, and the hills had seemed to agree with this because they were shaped so. She looked back again and saw her track aligned with the river—but against the way of its movement, as though in contrary or complement, she knew not. She did not know these words in any language. She knew patterns, rhythms, sensations, mind pictures, scarcely any emotion, no philosophy, right-nor-wrong doing. Simple words. Pain. She knew pain, simple words. Pain came with people. Pain came with mishappening things—stones falling, feet slipping on stone, a mishandling of the awl. Pain could not be recalled, was forgotten. Was not except when it lingered or came again in a pattern.

Late in the day... the stream she now felt to follow the sun's invisible trail.

She had eaten little all day, small curled emerging fern heads in flat moist places streamside, and a bit of the pemmican she almost always had in her pouch. That was most sustaining, tasty with fat and dried roast meal, nutmeat and dried berries, several kinds. But it would not last. She did not think of it. It was to hand or not when needed. That was *all*.

The girl had followed the sinuous day-long stream valley until its tributary crossings, hitherto small, met with a larger. She stood looking upstream there, at both streams. She followed the smaller. It felt right.

The hills went lower, the sky in its leaving light closer. She came to another stream, joining, also smaller than this, the latest sinew of drawing forth through a pattern. She went upstream, it narrowed and laughed with her, bubbling. She looked around suddenly, stood as a stock, stopped looking. She was the fawn again.

They did not care if she perceived them. Young scouts of True People, but very few, had come after her, for the joy and because it must be. The tracking of youths, mere boys, was good practice but she was not tolerable quarry, they thought; not even as deer to be watchful and careful. Though she could stand invisible were she so moved, they knew it of her. The scout boys came on, playing the day long, down the river and up the creek, tracking her. Stopping at vines hanging down through the trees, swinging and dropping; stopping at rocks jutting, jumping to the swimming hole; stopping to tickle the river trout—always half-mindfully following the girl.

Brown with faint moony glimmers, between gray-seeming gently greening slopes, the stream now was small, scarcely wide enough for her length athwart. Still she followed. It was thickly wooded country, small slopes. She followed not far before finding the black shadow on her left hand. Feet dripping, she climbed out toward it and sat down against the shadowy rock-ledge. Here it was very dark, almost black. She lay curled against it, facing the hard bosom. She reached round and over the rough surfaces, her hand seeking the crevice where the cattail lay. But found it not. She had forgotten the place, had never known it. This was not where the cattail was hidden, but some other rock, some otherwhere in another pattern. She had been like the stars to move places in the warp and weft while she slept, but she had moved out of her own familiar pattern and now had not the cattail to fondle, had not the kind pale face to recall in the dream.

The boy-voices, speaking True People (led by Red Fox), had ceased distant murmuring. There were no canoe deeps on the little stream. But she was not thinking of it. She was sleeping. The pattern was set to change again. There would be a newer, stranger way.

Pilot of Varying Lights

Sam Knightlinger, a man with short cropped black hair, rich black skin, and a calm manner—new director of crew operations—was observing the men and women seated at rows of display monitors in the humming NASA control center. Coffee in hand, he walked from station to station, listening to conversations between controllers and astronauts from sources as distant as Mars, the moon and Earth Island—the planet's first permanent orbiting space colony. Hearing a buzz among the controllers near the door, he looked back. He understood that it would be difficult getting a feel for the normal run of things today: A small group led by his supervisor had just come in and was converging on him through various aisles in the room.

Brisk and neat Della Swift, head of colony coordination, came up and touched his arm. "Sam, I want you to meet—"

Knightlinger thrust out his hand. "—Dr. Ardley, of course. I've seen you in holo."

Ardley hesitated pointedly then shook his hand. "We haven't met—So let the lady finish the introductions, all right?" Ardley was was tanned and reddish-blond, crisp and assured.

As was her way, Della managed a wry yet sorry smile for Sam. "This is Sam Knightlinger, new director of crew-op. Dr. Ardley and his assistants will be in and out the next few weeks, Sam—rushing to finalize plans and gear up for Island 2."

"Fine, Della." He made what could pass for a welcoming gesture then walked away.

Della Swift looked after with regret. Later she would excuse Ardley: "An arrogant son of a bitch, yes, but brilliant. They have pardon and they know it." Now she turned to Ardley. "Guess you'll have to help yourself. You've been in before."

Ardley smiled, taking her arm. "I prefer your assist to his anyway. Mind?"

Across the busy room and sipping lukewarm coffee, Sam continued his round, keeping clear of the little knot of engineers. Definitely *beige*, that man. Nope—should not let him get to me. He stopped short behind a balding controller whose voice was suddenly raised in agitation. Knightlinger put his hand on the man's shoulder.

He looked up. "Maj. Bishop's—lost his suit pressure—Capt. Boehme's up there alone in the shuttle."

"Gi'me," said Knightlinger, taking the headset from the controller. He remembered the name: She had authored a paper on intuition in space, something as yet untested. Evidence was anecdotal. Most astronauts, especially the scientists among them, now shied away from discussing it.

"Capt. Boehme, this is Knightlinger—director of crew-op." He had yet to meet Rebecca Boehme. His tone was firm and, he hoped, reassuring. "Tell me everything that's happened up there. Are you in command of the vehicle?"

He paused for an answer, his fingers absently brushing through his lightless kinky hair. Then her quiet voice sounded, as though coming not from space but the center of his mind.

~~~~~~~~

From the table in his palm-shaded backyard, Sam Knightlinger sat gazing at Rebecca Boehme's cap of brassy hair. His glance slipped to her fine-boned pensive face as she studied her preflight checklists. Twilight was deepening, yet she continued reading the lighted characters of the small display. He was disappointed with the tiny device held in her thin hands. *Glance up right now, you might catch something of yourself in my eyes.*

He reached for his wine glass, feeling foolish. He had hoped to expand her borders and lay them with colors. All the hues of intimate encounter. For months he had wanted to feel only Rebecca—around
~~~~~~~~

him, above him, beneath him. But it wasn't going to happen. He sighed, drank the wine.

Maybe Bishop's ghost was still hanging around, anyway. Little more than ten months had passed. She was concentrating now on recovery from a breakdown, on retraining, thoroughly occupied with her goal of returning to space. And Rebecca had something to overcome. She had both piloted and commanded missions before this loss of confidence. In some circles there was still speculation about her readiness. Most found her lacking in toughness, weak even. Too fragile for the job.

"More wine, Bo?"

She looked up, smiling. "Mmm."

He tipped the dark merlot into her glass. The ground shook. Down coast, as they watched, a night flight lifted off in a cloud of light. They looked at one another.

"Just 39 hours, babe."

Rebecca's slight answering smile did not match the intensity of her gaze.

Locking Capt. Boehme's helmet in place, Knightlinger smiled some encouragement. Through the dark reflecting faceplate he failed to make out her high cheekbones and what he knew of her serious expression. She acknowledged with thumbs-up that the suit's systems were go. He moved around to secure the helmet over the other crew member's more symmetrical features. The young pilot, Lt. Aiko Tsuchi, was about to make her second orbital flight, a supply run to NASA's space station within the geosynchronous orbit.

Sam stood a moment, smiling down confidence upon his friend before turning to climb out the hatch.

Preflight jitters had been flitting within, preoccupying her, but now she watched as the man disappeared. Like one coming out through foggy dreams to find the morning, she said, "Did you see that, Win?"

"—Pardon, Commander?" There was trepidation in the answering female voice.

Shrinking, Rebecca made no answer.

The minutes passed as they continued checking onboard systems. T-minus five minutes. Commander Capt. Boehme and pilot Lt. Tsuchi studied the data displays and control banks around them, reviewing the positions of overhead toggles. T-minus 5 seconds. Capt. Boehme give computer command and the three main engines below started with a mighty bang. The solid rocket boosters boomed to life. A slight vibration.... Gripping the arms of her seat, Rebecca tensed as the tower of pad B went slowly past the wraparound windows above. Then, accelerating with sickening force, bucking and twisting, the shuttle rolled, pitched, yawed into the once familiar east-northeast Gibraltar course.

Far away and below, from an observation deck on the ground, Sam Knightlinger shaded his eyes and watched the flashing white point of the STS, tethered to its pale yellow flame and billowing contrail, until it disappeared through distant skies.

Clean black space, with its mental and spiritual healing, Bo .... Get you some and bring it back in your eyes.

They were only 126 seconds into the flight and already 43 kilometers out. The orange flame of the eight booster separators engulfed the crew's wraparound windows. Six seconds more—the boosters were gone, gravity sucked. The ride smoothed out but they did not relax. Watching the data displays, Boehme said, "Pressing to MECO."

"Roger, Commander." Thrust of excessive gravity prevented the pilot from glancing toward the captain. *I hope you're ready, Commander. Because the official line won't save us now.*

Feeling leaden, several times their normal weight, they were reaching for main engine cut off at orbital velocity.

The fuels in their external tank now expended, the orbiter pitched over, leveling off. There flowed blue curving earth out their windows. Rebecca's heart filled at the sight. Aiko Tsuchi monitored the sequence as onboard computers disengaged their orbiter from the great external tank. Three red lights on the panel before the pilot went out. Now the orbital maneuvering system's thrusters began firing for the final nudge into orbit. Heaviness fell away, as finally topping the orbit, they lightened to nothing.

The pair removed their helmets, and Rebecca saw Tsuchi's face slightly flattened, her ponytail drifting out like strands of black seaweed. With a pang of joy, she experienced anew the sensation of weightlessness. But the buoyant emotion was instantly quelled, as the specter of Win Bishop's body—afloat against fathomless blackness, his suit deflated—flashed into her mind.

Zero gravity. Major Winston Bishop, mission commander, was preparing to leave the orbiter to work on its robotic arm. The arm had malfunctioned just as they were extending it to retrieve one of the European Space agency's orbiting bio-labs.

I'll have that thing operational in no time, Bo.

They were suited and helmeted, floating on opposite sides of the sealed airlock hatch. *Monitor me. And don't forget, the sound of your larynx vibrating in my helmet excites me.*

She smiled, aware of the broad grin behind his obscuring faceplate. *Phooey. Think I'll report you.*

Winston Bishop chuckled. *Phooey? Better watch that language. I guess commanding that last mission went to your head. You forgot how to take orders, pilot.*

Rebecca said, *Orders? Phooey.*

She heard his answering chuckle. All good-natured, professional. Everything decent and orderly. The need for order out here was obvious. Bishop never lost that sense, was confident and reassuring under pressure. Yet, watching him check out a zero-torque drill, she recalled a time when he betrayed fear—in a flip remark comparing black holes to dark spots in the psyche. *Bottomless pits, right there in the soul.* (Grin.)

His back to her, Bishop was ready to exit the airlock.

Win! She called it out. *I've got an impression—you should use the MMU!*

The manned mobility unit, a backpack with encircling arms and powered by nitrogen thrusters, was something Bishop habitually refused when he had work that kept him in close range of the shuttle.

You can burn back here faster if anything goes wrong.

He turned about slowly. *Funny, a moment ago I felt the same thing.... But you know I prefer the tether.*

Tsuchi and Boehme had achieved a circular orbit, 210 kilometers out, when Rebecca unstrapped to come away from her seat. Moving the members of her body in unison, feet in the air and her short brassy hair fluffed out, she worked compulsively, loading the computers with instructions. To Tsuchi's discomfort, she said nothing as she began work.

Transporting a supply module, they were on target for the mission to NASA's "beehive," its network of floating stations and staging point for moon, geosynchronous, and libration flights. Tsuchi unstrapped and glanced at the taciturn commander, thinking, Unnerving, cold as Pluto in here. She slid to the after flightdeck to oversee the slow opening of the great payload bay doors. It was still a revelation to her, this view of shimmering azure atmosphere against blue-black space. The calm of infinity set her spirit strumming. Staring out, she mused on the peculiar notion, which some astronauts claim, that space carries promptings and peace unmuddied by earth's dense atmosphere. What did it mean?

She turned back to begin checking vehicular response, but found Capt. Boehme usurping this job.

What the hell am I supposed to do?

She arced into mid-deck to see if the equipment was secure. In the cabin she did a double-take on discovering a water drop, the size of an orange, forming on one side of the chlorination valve. If it grew too large, its molecular attractions might be disturbed enough to break. Dispersed water droplets, floating willy-nilly about in the craft, might short out onboard electronic systems. She spun away and the movement nauseated her.

Commander. She called weakly from the opening between compartments.

Shaking off her preoccupation, Rebecca turned slowly. *What is it, Aiko?*

There's a water ball in here. Her voice quavered with nausea. *Maybe we should contact our controller?* She knew it a measure of her *own* lack of confidence in this mission with her commander.

Rebecca slid past her to examine the globoid seepage on the valve. Already as big as a grapefruit. Boehme glanced at the toolkit secure among the equipment and Tsuchi, following her gaze, reached for it. *What do you need? She surveyed the neat array of zero-torque tools.*

Seven and W. Nausea gone? Rebecca drifted back to let her in. Pointing to the opening, she said, *Lock seven into the ratchet of W and insert it there. When you're tightly engaged, turn it maybe ninety degrees—right.*

Aiko did as instructed, and the seepage stopped. *Better gather that with something,* said Rebecca as she turned toward the flight deck.

Tsuchi got a towel out of the tiny locker and gingerly soaked up the water. When she re-entered the cockpit, Boehme was strapped in and studying earth through the wraparound windows. Lt. Tsuchi secured herself, and, following a few practice burns, settled the orbiter back into the proper attitude for the remainder of the climb.

Staring at the earth just before sunset, Rebecca's gaze was caught by smoking Mount Etna. A prickly infilling of the glands about her eyes ... the quick compression of her emotional heart.... She held her breath as the sun sank behind them.

Win Bishop opened the outer hatch, secured himself to a line, and slowly drifted for the robotic arm.

Where's my chatter? She heard him ask it where she floated behind the airlock hatch. The impression causing her apprehension continued with her, even as the view beneath open cargo bay doors stunned her anew with its display of the blue beauty of space curving beyond. *You look pretty good out there. What-a-view.*

Lifting out of the bay, he passed out along the mantis-like arm. Then he paused, apparently looking at the planet.

Rebecca glanced at the MMUs attached to the bulkhead outside the airlock. He always claimed that the unit hampered his movements. She watched him reach for a tool floating tethered at his side. Then she heard him gasp.

Oxygen pressure?! A malfunctioning regulator would deplete his suit pressure, boiling his blood. He made a small gesture. Her arm went out to open the hatch, but her limbs were numbing. Bumping the bulkhead she negotiated the airlock.... Scarcely she heard the soft *pfff* in her helmet ... saw his limbs blossom out.

She backed into the MMU and managed to release it. Fumbling to activate the nitrogen jet she felt it would never start, yet it fired and began propelling her towards him. Drawing up, she saw him outspread in the limp suit, floating like a flower on water. She turned for an instant. Smoking Mount Etna, on distant earth, met her bewildered gaze.

It's dark, Commander, urged the pilot still strapped in beside her. Their cabin lights were out but the data displays glowed. Then, *Look! A night flight!*

Through the wraparound windows Aiko and Boehme watched the fire of rockets from earth, winking, emerging through the atmosphere.

Wonder whose? said the pilot as the light moved in the blackness of earth's shadowed bottom until it went out in the east. *Bet it's a Fly-back F-1. That looked like the fire of SSMEs.*

The radio light came on in the panel. Rebecca flipped a switch, acknowledging.

Sam here, came the friendly voice from earth. *How you doin'?*

The voice gave her a welcome rush of inner sights: Good humored dark eyes, sea breezes, red wine under palms.

Pretty good here, Sam. Had a leak in the chlorinator valve. Lt. Tsuchi corrected it. We've got lights out and are cruising in the dark at about 300km altitude. I see Delphinus—I think it is—outside my window, and in the east we just had unidentified rocket fire. Know whose? Over.

That would be China with spare parts for Island 2. You skipped by that valve leak pretty fast, babe. Care to tell yo' pappy what happened?

Boehme chuckled and asked Tsuchi to fill him in.

Then the director of crew-op came back, saying, *Uh—We have a complication with one of ESA's communications satellites....* Already she felt her heart beating as he continued. *You may be uneasy ... I understand, Bo, but there's no one else around and I know you can handle it. Why not give Aiko her head on this one?*

Rebecca was silent. Then she acknowledged, and his briefing followed. Capt. Boehme signed off and, ignoring Sam's advice, ordered the pilot to turn on the overhead and start work on the coordinates. The commander unstrapped to prepare for extravehicular activity. She did not want a crewmember doing this walk.

Working on the coordinates Lt. Tsuchi said with deceptive evenness, *I'd like to do that EVA, commander.* But the other continued mid-deck. *Capt. Boehme.... Now Aiko spoke a note of warning: I'd be alone here, if anything ... happened.*

It was manipulative but it worked.

Adrift in the cabin Rebecca swung about slowly, staring at her, vaguely reliving the nightmare of isolation.... Of traveling high above earth, repairing the robot arm—her own commander's body strapped to his seat in the cockpit. She fought the futility of trying to save either of them from her fears. Life had moved on, leaving both Win Bishop and her personal experience in some place she kept trying to call the past.

The craft and its lone space walker were in sunlight, the earth above glowing and milky white. Boehme watched Tsuchi on a display as the other ghosted toward the target; wearing the MMU and trailing a thin cloud of ice crystals.

It's a miracle out here, came Aiko's murmur inside Rebecca's helmet. Wearing the suit was a precaution taken in case she was needed out there.

Your suit systems, camera, and MMU are all reading fine, pilot.

Hovering near the spherical satellite, Aiko did not respond. Then, *Looks like part of quadrants two and three have been strafed by dust or something. Did you just see some of its particles disperse?*

Boehme glanced reflexively at the neighboring monitor. *Negative. I was watching you, not your pictures. Anything else?*

The rest of the satellite appears operable, but maybe these pix'll show something. Aiko said this coming around the sphereoid into full view of the shuttle's monitoring camera.

OK, c'mon back and I'll send the data to Sam.

But Tsuchi had stopped near the satellite. *Roger, that.* But she did not move.

C'mon.

I can't. The control's disengaged.

Well, keep trying. I'm coming out.

Capt. Boehme unstrapped and slid to the airlock.

Outside she donned an MMU, ignited the tiny rockets, and glided past the supply module in the bay. Coming up on the stranded pilot, reversing rockets, she saw Aiko fiddling with the control on an arm of the unit. Rebecca reached to grasp the stick and felt it slip loosely from side to side. She started removing the housing, but stopped.

She seemed poised, as though listening. With Tsuchi wondering.

Go out! Quickly! I'll push you.

She grabbed the arm of the unit and began propelling her around the satellite. She circled widely, doubling their distance to the shuttle.

Aiko felt her fear coming true: Boehme was dangerously unstable.

Commander, why are we going <u>away</u> from the orbiter?!

Although seeming a void of motionless peace, orbital space is pocked with moving particles unchecked by friction, bits of debris and junk moving at tens of thousands of kilometers per hour. Before Rebecca could answer, a blinding flash blossomed where the satellite had been, sending silent reflecting radiance and fragments out through the corridor between spacewalkers and aircraft. In its rush of light their eyes were momently blinded.

Aiko breathed out her wonderment in silence. Was this it—the intuition?

How did you know, Commander?

The pressurized suit hid the other's shrug.

I knew.

The STS was soft-docking at the beehive. Sunlight glinted off banks of solar arrays as they passed into the docking sphere of one cylindrical station. The station spun slowly about its axis to provide .1 G—just enough gravity to keep coffee in cups and people in touch with the floor. The two astronauts checked in at the nearly empty flight desk to file their reports. On duty the dark young man with an engaged glance looked at the transcripts on the display. He exclaimed over the mishap. Meteoroid or space junk hits weren't unknown, but they were rare.

"Your ID says you're rated for inter-orbital flight, Capt. Boehme," said the man as he turned away from the monitor. "We've got an unscheduled trip to Earth Island, if you're interested. If you're too tired, I'll see who else I can scrounge up."

Rebecca turned to Aiko. "Want to pick up a pile of hours in the IOTV?"

The other's face lit up in the affirmative, emphasizing her beautiful horizontal features. She had yet to visit the elegant celestial city of space.

The young man glanced at the UT clock. "Give you an hour to rest up, then I've got to get Dr. Gas on the sling."

"Dr. Gas?" asked Tsuchi.

"The Very Great Architect of the Islands hisself." He looked down his nose at them, nostrils flaring.

"His self," laughed Rebecca. To Tsuchi she added, "I don't think he likes my ideas—if that's the word for them."

"On what?"

"Space intuition."

"Is it ESP?"

"May be. But I don't call it that because it mixes it up with something else. It is discernment *and* extra to the senses yet completely relevant to them. Anyway, I have no scientific curiosity about it anymore." She said softly as though to herself, "Wish I hadn't written that paper."

"Ride should be interesting, then," the amused young man said with a smile. "They're throwing 'luncheon' for him day after tomorrow. Better grab a sandwich and get some rest." He gestured toward the hatch, which led through compartments to the snack area, "Soy sloppy joes today!"

Aiko giggled as they stepped lightly through the hatch. "Yummy."

"Yummy?—soy sloppy joes?"

"Not them." She looked back, flashing a smile over her shoulder at the man behind the desk.

They rocketed through the flashing radioactive Van Allen belt in the inter-orbital transport vehicle. Rebecca, her hair fluffed out, and Aiko, whose ponytail drifted, were at the consoles; the astrophysicist strapped in behind them. His blond hair always closely cropped—warding the foolishness of zero gravity—astute, self-assured, Dr. Chaunce Ardley listened with polite attention as Tsuchi described the destruction of ESA's satellite by the meteoroid.

Remarkable. But Capt. Boehme is a remarkable woman. I was in flight-com the day you made your heroic deorbit. His manner was lightly ironic, his voice smooth as satin.

Feeling heat rise in her face, Rebecca turned back to the panel.

Ardley continued. *Really, how did you know you and the lieutenant were in danger?*

Skimming the data displays, her back still to him, she wanted to say, "The Easter Bunny told me." But lightly she said, *Rather not say.*

He moved smoothly on. *Now you have piqued my curiosity of course. I've heard of space intuition, but we haven't studied it yet ... not seriously. Until we do—it does not exist. You swim, Capt. Boehme.*

Mmm. She nodded.

Good. He lit a gold-colored cigarette, murmuring, *It'll filter out OK. You don't mind do you?... We'll go swimming at the Lunar Club. You'll come, too, Lieutenant.*

Tsuchi laughed, recognizing the afterthought. *No thanks, got to do my nails.*

His eyes steeped in cigarette smoke, the physicist smiled.

The great mottled dome of the moon was out their windows on the left. In time a speck of light to the right began steadily growing. Later, as they drew near, it outshone the constellations, a shining great wheel—full of life. This great colony, held in place by the gravity of heavenly bodies, swung slowly, majestically, like a great spoked wheel in space. The vast mirrors, reflecting its image above, provided solar light and energy.

Tsuchi pointed out a shield of rock—slag from the furnace that was located ten km south of the torus. *Fly past the furnace and hover,* commanded Ardley. *We'll watch those mass-catchers dock.*

Out the window they saw two massive, grid-covered Kevlar bags, full of moon rock, preparing to dock at the furnace. Glistening clumps of raw ore, floating in space, awaited the refining process that would extract glass, iron, titanium, magnesium, aluminum, all for use in building Island 2. Stacks of refined sheet metals, waiting for a tow to the fabrications sphere, were suspended beyond the glowing furnace.

We've just begun coating the new island with aluminum extracted from that ore. Another year and we'll have our second self-supporting colony. Rocket up to it, will you Capt. Boehme.

She turned to Aiko. *Take us on through Earth Island's spokes, close to the torus, and you'll get a glimpse into it before we go on to the fabrications sphere.*

Tsuchi inverted the vehicle and flew across the secondary mirrors and louvered shields covering the outer surface of the vast torus. Through the slanted shields she saw green and yellow fields, fountains, sheep grazing. A tiny gasp escaped her lips and she glanced at Ardley.

He smiled.

Gerard O'Neill and his students designed the colony decades ago. My uncle was one of those students, and he inspired me. Invert again and you'll see her new sister.

They drew slowly up past the fabrications sphere, above the hub of the torus. Further out they saw the skeletal structure of Island 2, the plastic-covered ribs of its torus, spokes, and hub revolving in space. Leading up to it from the fabrications sphere was a long vibrating hose. A conical vehicle attached and acting as a nozzle sprayed the skeletal torus with gleaming metal.

Ardley continued his smooth tutorial, saying, *The sheet aluminum we saw beside the furnace is boiled to vapor and shot through the nozzle under pressure. It hardens instantly on the shell.*

The two women murmured appropriately. It was not unexpected that such murmuring his due.

Undressing for her swim, Rebecca wondered why she bothered with him. Ardley was attractive and repellent in the same glance. She tried picturing him as a down and out failure. She chuckled. Chaunce Ardley with slumping shoulders and fraying cuffs.

She stepped from the women's lounge in a skimpy one-piece. Bright, laughing, sophisticated people clustered about the vast pool, solar bathing. Uh-oh.... Agoraphobia. Wrong turn. Better go back. It came swiftly to her that space was where she belonged—not society. But she could not have the first without that community. In polarity was the holding together—and the struggle to part.

In silver boxer trunks, his physique tan and sleek, Ardley approached. "Care for a drink, Rebecca?"

Charming smile. He's going to be nice. "Maybe a little chablis." She followed to the bar.

They took their drinks to the edge of the pool, refreshening their feet in its pink waters. A stream of Chaunce's friends and hangers-on came and went. Faint smiles crossed Rebecca's features and vanished. A lull came and Ardley set down his glass.

"Don't look so miserable, Rebecca."

There was an embarrassed pause. She might have brought up her breakdown as an excuse ... but she knew better. She was out of her zone—that was all.

He gave her a casual but sensual smile and squeezed her thigh before plunging into the rose-tinted waters. Burnished with red-gold hair, his body glistened up at her. Came an impulse to hurry away confusingly combined with a desire to stay and swim beside that attractive form. She sighed, downed her wine and stood uncertainly. He beckoned and she dove, meeting him under water.

Chaunce took her arm and pointed downward. She looked and saw the shell-strewn bottom. The two dove deeper and began plucking shells to carry away. They surfaced in a welter of pink bubbles and swam for the shady end of the pool. There they lined up their find according to species.

Delighted, she held up a yellow sunray Venus. "Imagine transporting all these from the planet!"

"My compliments." He cocked his head in a mock bow.

She smiled. No modesty, false or otherwise, here.

Suddenly he slapped his neck, swearing in irritation. "I didn't import that!"

"A mosquito!" Pure glee in her response. And happy pride.

"Don't look so damned pleased. Some cow-brained joker has spoiled the paradisal softness of the place."

Rebecca's face flooded. She managed a weak smile. My cow-brained compliments. Shortly after the island's christening she had brought in a few vials of various insects, pupae and larvae, on one of her supply flights. Finding the mosquitos thriving after her long absence prompted the joyous outburst. Now she fervently hoped that the predators she had planted, the spiders and damselflies, were doing as well.

Chaunce misread her flaming features, and made a curt apology. "Maybe they came on some plants—I hate seeing this perfection marred."

Out of the memory of her sorrow, she asked, "Couldn't there be purpose, a ... sort of redeeming purpose ... in imperfection?" She offered it with a tentative smile. His face darkened. He was going to retort, but impulsively she slipped beneath the mild waters.

Piqued, he pursued. But as they swam she thought of Sam and found herself suddenly weary of Ardley, bone-tired as well. They surfaced, and, pleading exhaustion after the grueling flights of the past two days, she excused herself. He was rebuffed, irked, but, before she had gathered her things, was receiving the attentions of another.

Aiko was out. Rebecca stood on the balcony, gazing across the park. Path lights were on, enhancing the artificial night. The ring of secondary mirrors in space, just above the residential level, were turned so that solar light from the giant mirror was deflected. The still air was apple-blossom scented. It was late, not many were stirring. One couple was descending the stairs leading to a suite among the larger terraced apartments on her left. Familiar—the long dark hair of the woman....

Lamplight from the landing cast a glow on the man's blond head. Hand in hand, Aiko and Chaunce Ardley slipped into the suite.

That's that.

Casual sex always seemed incongruous, anyway. To find the intimate places and call forth pleasure, hands had to be not just any hands, but hands attached to a body full of a particular soul. It might have been Win Bishop.... —The MMU probably would not have saved him anyway.... *The sadness again.*

But now thoughts of Sam Knightlinger's kindness and friendly smile surfaced. Musing and wistful, she turned and went inside.

Troubled, Rebecca tossed on the daybed in the darkened room. She rolled on her side, her stomach, her back. Her conscience was uneasy ... pestered. *What is it!?* —the mosquitos!

She sat up rubbing her brow. *If the balance isn't there ... more pests than predators?...*

She closed her eyes, frowned, lay back and plucked at the sheet. *When will I learn discretion, cease careless presumption?*

Morning, and she was preparing to visit space. It was close to noon when, suited and carrying her helmet for the walk, she entered the docking lobby. Without gravity here at the hub, Rebecca grabbed the rail, pressing her Velcro soles into the Velcro carpeting, moving slowly to the flight desk.

Hearing a commotion she turned from the woman at the desk to see a group step from the tube and gingerly enter the lobby. Fifteen or twenty suited tourists, caring helmets and led by a young guide, came toward the desk. All were excited, laughing. The woman at the desk smiled at her.

EMU touring today. Vacationers want to walk in space.

In the docking area, Rebecca donned an MMU, fired it and did test maneuvers. Then she burned away, crossing over the torus where, below, the Lunar Club had its halcyon view of space. She glanced into the posh room far below where Dr. Ardley would soon be feted.

Rebecca inverted and watched the slow revolution of the new Island, the brilliant aluminum drenching by the conical vehicle and hose from the fabrications sphere. Then, burning away, she headed into the deepness. Faintly flashing as she flew, cosmic particles darted across her retinas. Particles, particles, she mused, Everything is particles. People are particles. Gulfs and particles.

Now, thrusters off, floating in the cosmic atmosphere of stars, Rebecca saw the fulgent sun, a great star in the darkness of space. Beneath it hung the fragile half-planet earth—a fair, sapphire foot-stool. Opposite earth stood the moon with its bright white top, its bottom shaded and pocked green in the pale earthshine. All silent fragile spheres, every one. And surrounding them rode the monstrous, bright but navigable stellar network—devised, fused and piloted by a Mind and Force beyond human comprehension.

Reversing to a standstill, Rebecca felt herself caught in this divine snare of varying lights. She was organized stardust and soul, known through and through by the Pilot, drifting in the Pilot's measureless sea of star particles. She was silent, tipping in the presence of Silence.

Now, lighter yet surer than touch, guidance pressed gently on her spirit.

And she was disquieted. Heart thumping, Rebecca Boehme ghosted back toward the distant islands where two great wheels turned slowly, solemnly, in space. As she flew, Rebecca noticed the MMU tourists in that distance, hovering like bees along one side of the protracted hose. The nozzle vehicle was spraying the hull of the new torus in bright aluminum.

Then, even as she burned toward them. Then. Vapor under tremendous pressure burst from the hose near its couplings. Rebecca gasped as the wild white gas blew away the group that had gathered so close—a soundless explosion sending its members spinning wildly out. Out out into the fathomless ocean of space.

She chose one and fired after it but, unable to match the speed of the tiny sliver vanishing far ahead, she turned about searching for others. Too late. They were all shot out into black space on a ride eternal.

Her own oxygen pressure was almost gone. Stiff with anguish, she headed for the docking area. The blow of gas had ceased, its delivery hose empty, gaping, eerily afloat. Approaching the docks, she saw a score of vehicles preparing to rocket away on a hopeless quest.

At Kennedy Space Center Launch Complex 14, Sam Knightlinger left control and walked rapidly down the hall to his office. He went to the window and stood staring out at the canal basin where two dozen external tanks sat on barges, waiting to be towed to one of the vehicle assembly buildings. He smoothed his moustache and brushed absently through the wiry hair at his temples. News of the tragedy at Earth Island had just come down. He pictured her serious features, those still hazel eyes. Sam Knightlinger drummed his fingers on the window frame.

C'mon, kid. Get your butt back on this planet.

Draped over the foamed-in couch, clutching some pillows, Rebecca stared vacantly. Aiko was out. It was almost time to rocket back to the beehive and then on to Earth, but she lay staring without seeing the ponytail palm beneath a skylight in a high curve of the foamed-in white wall. Her eyes were puffy, a tear stood on her lash. She felt the hand of sorrow hovering, poised to push down on her again.

An electronic monotone voice hummed into the quiet, announcing visitors. Tiny, lucent holo-images of Lt. Tsuchi and Chaunce Ardley were displayed in a curve of the room. Rebecca spoke, the door slid open. She sat up, slowly, fluffing her short hair was nervous fingers.

"The rescue vehicles are back," said Tsuchi. "We'll never see those tourists again."

Still wearing the silver textelite suit he had been feted in, Dr. Ardley wore a grim preoccupied expression. Feeling Rebecca's gaze on him, he exerted himself to smile and sit down beside her on the couch. She wondered idly what he was doing here: He would surely be staying to begin at least the appearance of an investigation.

"You're okay aren't you, Rebecca?" The show of concern grated falsely on her. She looked at him, quietly. Restive, he stood and walked the small space. Aiko hesitated, looking from one to the other, then slid onto a couch opposite Rebecca. No one spoke.

Rebecca's statement surfaced into the silence: "You didn't do adequate stress tests on that hose?... Or there was something else ... something neglected."

Chaunce stopped, looked at her, eyebrows raised. "Star knowledge again, Rebecca?"

He continued pacing. Of course he truly had misjudged it. But the engineers should have been more vigilant. The technicians could have caught the error. The damned tour group shouldn't have been up against it.

He glanced smiling at Lt. Tsuchi, ignoring her bewilderment, then said to Rebecca, "I wouldn't spread that around.... The perception, or question even, of your fitness for space.... There is no evidence on which to base those *false* accusations."

"Not yet." *Pressing ahead you imagine cosmic dread won't bring you downward into its orbit. —The abyss of light unfathomable. Unfathomable of what Is.*

He looked away, relieved that he had taken the trouble to change the data. His holo camera on the hose, as well as a score of other shortcuts.... The budget—the deadline—none of this had allowed for anything else.

"You'll be wanting to get back to Kennedy," he said smoothly, smiling at Lt. Tsuchi's confusion. "Or, you can visit a while longer with me. Rebecca is quite capable of the flight back." He turned and left the tiny suite.

The onboard computers were programmed for reentry. Orbiting blue earth, tailfirst and upside down, they are pressure-suited and strapped in. Lt. Tsuchi fired the OMS engines for the tug needed to slow the craft into elliptical orbit. The radio light came on. Rebecca flipped the switch. *Boehme,* she said.

Sam here. How's it going? Ready to deorbit?

Affirmative.... Dr. Ardley's negligence was responsible for the accident at Earth Island.

There was silence in her helmet. She waited. Then he said, *He has already radioed and said you might suggest something like that.*

No proof, Sam. That I know.

Again there was silence.

It won't hold up, Rebecca.

I'm aware of that.

So what are you going to do?

Nothing. That is, I've already done it in telling him. And you.

—Right. Well, don't worry, there will be an investigation. You coming in now?

Want me in?

God, yes.

She detected the presence of his lopsided sexy grin.

I've got the runway down here carpeted in red.

Got wine?

Everything, babe.

Sam Knightlinger left control and strode down the hall. On his way out to the runway he pictured peace in Rebecca's eyes, before hurrying on to the rest of her.

MORE S. DORMAN SCIENCE FICTION
From

SiXPointZ HiTopOLis

It was 1900 A.D.

They were gathered round the z-pod in Tu's hand. Huddling with the FivePoints 2017 CE gang, by a stone wall of the dark Akropolis Cemetery, HBBBAH rubbed the sweat out of his dark broom'do. He looked about him with that special CossycSystems eye of his. He said with disgust, "A line of 0's and 1's."

Pomala, the albino girl with blue tattooed face, smiled off into the pod-lit dark, saying, "Or, x's and o's!"

Eyes zoned in concentration, fringe of black hair hanging over his symmetrical Osiian features, Tu had again worked the Hadesthon calculations. He worked them just as the battery gave out. The game display was suddenly dark. Disconcertingly so to the other five gang members. The battery was dead. And the cemetery around them, which they had not been attending to while gathered round the z-pod, was dark like a pit surrounded by hidden fire. Gaslight and some thin old-fashioned household electric glowed down from beyond the walls. On the west side, great monoliths of high school and church hunkered as black shadows.

Outside the Cemetery stood the venerable neighborhood of Five Points Akropolis 1900 A.D., rhythmic that evening, with nightlife of horse-and-carriages, pool halls, bars, and neighborhood sociability ebbing and flowing—including a game of kick-the-can. Certain areas of the city had been in tumult but it seemed quieter now, the riots perhaps abating. Remote fiddling and the tinkling of an upright piano drifted to them. The gang from FivePoints 2017 CE were wearing their jackets again, full of hope. Ready for November, 2017 CE—the fresh twinkle in time, courtesy (they were hoping) of the Hadesthon. Longing for streaming, games, apps and naChooos.

As the pod flicked off, Tu felt a great elation and would have jumped in the air and floated, hovering and gently crowing the fact. But he was Tu, so instead he said only, "Got it. And just in time."

He explained. "Nothing to do with the calculations, but this one glitch kept happening. Shooting Baltoid on Persesus29 fails the first five times, every time, then launches the P29 module gimmex.lld, causing bribell27.xee to gobble mega percentages of its CUP sickles—well, not mega, but you know what I mean."

"Sure we do" said HB.

The six members of FivePoints 2017, including Fabian, Quadri and Jayrai, scrambled for the wall to sit in line, await the recall in Time. Shyly, feeling just a bit weird and surprised by the suggestion, they held hands. Then maneuvered for position. Conversation happened.